D1487727

Finding A Loyal Love
2

A Novel By

A'Zayler

Text LEOSULLIVAN to 22828 to join our mailing list!

To submit a manuscript for our review, email us at leosullivanpresents@gmail.co

Chapter 1

It seemed as if the party was moving in slow motion as Kyle tried to get to Lay-Lay. She had been rapping and mean mugging Alissa and Candice for pretty much the entire song. He knew Lay-Lay, and he was actually surprised that she hadn't exploded on the two women already. Shalaya had told him about their little incident in the hospital the other day, and now this. Between him bringing Alissa to his sister Morgan's baby shower and Candice approaching him and Lay-Lay at the mall, he was sure she'd had enough of the two women.

The interaction had looked like child's play at first, but clearly that was no longer the case. He'd been watching the entire exchange from across the room. He and his boys had thought it was funny at first, until he noticed Lay-Lay headed towards Candice and Alissa. He moved as quick as he could to get in front of her. When he reached her, he stopped and grabbed both of her hands, only for her to snatch away.

"Move out my way."

"Nope. Come dance with me."

"I know you saw your little fan club trying me. Those bitches better pipe down before I beat their asses." Kyle ignored her and kissed her instead.

Surprisingly, the night had gone exceptionally well. After her small run in with Kyle's groupies, he and her had danced and enjoyed the party. It took him a few minutes to get her calmed down, but she eventually let it go. She made sure to mug both of those bitches whenever she caught them staring, but that was it. Kyle wouldn't let her do anything else. It had started getting late, so they were getting ready to leave. They made it out of the door before Alissa followed them out and called Kyle's name. He tried to ignore her, but she kept calling him. Lay-Lay was two seconds off her ass, but she decided to let Kyle handle his hoe.

"Just give me the keys. I'll wait for you in the car"

"You sure?"

"Yep. Make it quick. I'm not waiting that long."

She took the keys and headed in the other direction. The only thing she heard was Alissa ask why he'd been ignoring her before she was out of earshot. When she was comfortable in the passenger seat of his truck, she watched them through the windshield. She could tell whatever Alissa was saying was annoying Kyle. His face was frowned up, and he wasn't saying much. His body language screamed that he wasn't interested in anything she was saying. He stood there for another five minutes before he was headed in her direction. Alissa stood there looking defeated. She looked so pitiful that Lay-Lay almost felt bad for her. *Almost!* When Kyle got into the truck, he looked at her for a minute. She knew he was trying to see if she was mad, but she wasn't.

"Don't be staring at me trying to see if I'm mad," Lay-Lay looked at him.

"I don't care if you mad."

"That's what your mouth say. You better be glad I know you ain't worried about that bitch."

Kyle chuckled as he backed out of the parking spot. "If I was?"

"I would have beat both of y'all the fuck up."

"Lay-Lay, you wild as hell, mama," Kyle rested his hand on her thigh and gave it a light squeeze.

"You like it."

He winked at her. "I damn sure do."

They continued on their way until they returned to his house. They showered and got into bed. Lay fell asleep first. Kyle stayed awake watching her. He knew time was winding down, and he was going to have to tell her about his deployment soon. He hoped she would be supportive as she'd been in the past.

*****

This can't be life. Lay-Lay watched Kyle's chest rise and fall from his breathing. It was 5:36 in the morning, and she was wide-awake. They had fallen asleep pretty late, so why on Earth was she up? Nonetheless, she was grateful for another day; another twenty-four hours she was able to spend with Kyle. He was so beautiful. His 6'6, 265-pound frame, along with his caring and compassionate ways made her fall more and more in love each day. There was nothing about him that she didn't love. The fact that he loved her despite of all her flaws was even better.

Ever since the day she first met him, they'd had a connection. It was funny to her how after all these years, previous relationships, and hardship after hardship, they continued to love one another. Never in a million years would she have ever thought that the love they shared could be this real. Sure, they'd had feelings for each other and made it clear that they loved one another, but being with him daily, actually being able to see and feel the love was a totally different thing.

Everybody's had that one person they say I love you to, even if they're only saying it because it sounds good. In a way, she thought that was her and Kyle. Saying I love you to him was more so out of habit than anything. This was because she had been in love with Smoke for so long that she hadn't given it much thought.

She figured the love they exchanged was real, but in a friendly kind of way. She hadn't known it was so far from a friendship until she'd gotten to South Carolina. These past couple of weeks showed her that she'd been living like hell while being with Smoke. Love wasn't supposed to be painful. It was supposed to pure, kind, and unconditional. The more Lay-Lay thought about it, the more it hurt. She had been playing herself all of this time. She couldn't understand, for the life of her, how she had allowed herself to become so wrapped up into Smoke. It was like she'd lost her entire identity, and had become what he'd made her. Who in the hell would have ever allowed a man to do half the things Smoke had done to her, and chose to stay? Not Shalaya Hardaway! Well, not the Shalaya Hardaway that she used to be anyways.

The new one, and the one she was currently trying to get away from, had been playing the fool for too long. It was time out for that. As Lay-Lay laid in bed with her head on Kyle's chest, she vowed to change her ways. His handsome face looked so peaceful. She couldn't possibly be the reason to cause him any pain. She admired everything he'd gone through just to make sure she was comfortable. Not to mention, the trouble he'd taken on to ensure her safety. Thinking back to that day, Lay-Lay began to feel like an idiot. She was about to blow her brains out about Smoke's cheating ass.
Lawd I was a fucking fool! Here she was a college graduate and soon-

to-be law student, losing her mind behind an ex-drug dealer. *Tuh!* Never again. She owed Jade and Morgan's ass a punch to the face for letting her be that big of fool. Morgan especially! She knew how wonderful of a man Kyle was all this time, and she let her carry on like one of those ratchet bitches from the hood. Both of them would be getting a piece of her mind when they woke up. Kyle was a successful trauma surgeon. A fucking Major in the Army! He was making plenty of money, and she was running behind Smoke with her tongue out like a little dumb puppy. Hell, Kyle matched her *fly*; he was who she should have been with all this time. Her brain had obviously gone blank the night she had met that nigga.

Whatever it was, it was over now! Smoke could never get the time day from her again. Having hoes coming to see him at the hospital, calling the police on her and shit–they were just all wrong for each other. Smoke was a sweet person and real cool to hang around, but that was about it. He would probably be her friend forever because of their history, but relationship-wise, that was definitely a done deal. Kyle stirred lightly in his sleep, jolting her from her thoughts. When she looked up, his eyes were open and he was looking at the ceiling. She didn't say anything for a minute, because she didn't know whether or not he knew she too was awake. His heart was beating faster against her ear than it had been before.

"Shalaya, I have something to tell you." Welp. Obviously he had known she was awake. She shifted up some in the bed so she could see him. She was still lying across his chest, but she was now resting her chin on it so they were face-to-face.

"What's going on?" She could feel his heart beating faster and faster; this was serious. She was nervous about what he was going to say. Anytime Smoke needed to talk to her, it was something serious, like she needed to go to the clinic and get tested or some shit like that. She hoped like hell it wasnt anything like that. "I hope it's not bad." Him not saying anything right away didn't help her nerves any. After a few more minutes, he began to talk.

"I love you and I want to get married."

Lay-Lay scrunched her face up in confusion. "Excuse me?"

"I want you to marry me," Kyle was staring at her.

This was so far from what she thought she was about to hear that it didn't make any sense. That was definitely not what she was expecting to hear. She honestly didn't even know how to respond to that. She sat straight up in bed, shielding her naked body with the sheet. She pulled her bonnet off her head and ran her hand through her tangled tresses.

If they were about to talk about being husband and wife, she didn't want to scare him away with that ugly ass bonnet. Her hair probably didn't look much better, but it had to be better than that god-forsaken bonnet. He sat up against the headboard with his bare chest on display. He ran his hands over his face before meeting her eyes.

"Say something, Shalaya."

"You want me to be your wife?" Lay-Lay pointed at her chest, as if there was anybody else in the room.

"Yes. I love you. I know it's sudden, but I want us to be married. You're the only woman that has remained a constant fixture in my life. No matter what I've gone through, you've always been there. I mean sure, we've been involved with other people, but the fact still remains that you and I have been together for years. This isn't as farfetched as it may sound."

"I know. You just caught me off guard with this one."

"If you'll agree to marry me, I promise you'll never see another unhappy day in your life. When I saw you with that gun to your head, I died a thousand times before I could get to you. I was so scared you were about to be gone before we ever got our chance. I know you remember what I told you that day. I was serious, bae. If that gun hadn't jammed and you'd killed yourself, I would have never been the same again. I would have never forgiven myself for taking so long to say what we both already know. "

Lay-Lay started crying as she remembered the words he'd yelled at her. *Let me make it better Shalaya. Give me your heart and I promise to make it stop hurting.* That was the darkest day of her life, and he was there. He was the light that she followed out of that darkness. He'd always been her saving grace. Kyle was a listening ear when necessary, and the best confidant she ever known. He scooted towards her on the bed and grabbed her hands when he noticed she was shaking. He kissed her lips before leaning over her to his nightstand. The black velvet box he retrieved made her tears flow faster.

"Marry me, Shalaya. We don't have to tell anyone until you're ready. As long as you and I know, that's all that matters to me."

She slowly began to nod her head yes. Before she could open her mouth to scream yes the way she wanted to, he was on her. He had dropped the ring on the bed, and had her body engulfed in the tightest hug she'd ever had. She didn't remember him hugging her this hard when she'd tried to kill herself.

"Thank you, Kyle. Thank you so much."

He pulled back so he was looking at her face. His furrowed brow showed confusion. "What you thanking me for?"

"For loving me. You showed me what real love is. I had no clue before now." She smiled, as did he. After he picked up the ring box that had fallen to the floor, he opened it and the diamonds almost blinded her. "Damn! That muthafucka pretty!"

"Watch your mouth, crazy ass girl," Kyle laughed as he slid the diamond encrusted band on her finger. It was a 24-carat Canary diamond ring. Lay-Lay's eyes practically bulged out of her head. She'd seen this same ring on Paris Hilton in a magazine a few weeks back.

"Now Kyle, I know you're making money and everything, but I ain't know you had it like this. This ring is big as hell, boy." He smiled bashfully as she admired the way it looked on her hand. There was no way in the world she was going to be able to hide this–not that she wanted to, but still.

"It looks good on you. Come take a shower with me," Lay-Lay looked from her ring to Kyle, then back again.

"I don't want no water in my ring. I'll wait right here until you get back."

Kyle laughed at her so hard before telling her the ring would be fine. It took a little more convincing, but she eventually gave in. That was the best shower/sex she'd ever had. When they were dried off and dressed, Lay plopped back down on the bed, marveling at her ring.

"I think that was the best sex I've ever had. It's probably because you're my fiancé now and not my boyfriend."

"I didn't know sex went according to relationship status."

"Yep. It does."

"Well, if sex is like that while you're my fiancée, I can't wait until you're my wife."

"Shalaya Taylor. That does sound nice, huh?"

"Sounds like the best thing I've heard in my entire life." Kyle leaned over the bed and kissed her mouth before telling her to get up and get dressed. She asked a thousand times where they were going, but he refused to tell her. Because she was so eager to see, she didn't dress up; she threw on a pair of sweatpants and a fitted tank top. After brushing her hair into a neat ponytail at the top of her head, she put on her earrings and grabbed her purse.

"I'm ready." Kyle looked at her as he tied the string on his shoes.

"Well let's go then." He was dressed just as casual as she was in sweats and a t-shirt. On his head, he wore a hat. They both grabbed their jackets and headed for the door. Lay-Lay tried to hold in her excitement as they drove. When they stopped at the hospital, Lay-Lay was a bit thrown off.

"Why are we at your job?"

"I need to grab something real quick, then we'll go. Come on." Kyle grabbed her hand and held it as they made their way inside. The rode the elevators until it came to a stop. Kyle made sure to keep her hand in his. He was too happy to let it go. Holding hands had always been one of his favorite things to do. The majority of the women he'd dated weren't too fond of him holding their hand everywhere they went, but Shalaya seemed to love it. He looked down at her as they walked through the hallway.   He laughed a little when he saw her looking at her ring. He was glad she was liked it, because it had cost a pretty penny. He'd used practically all of the money from his last deployment to buy it, and it was definitely worth it. He'd bought it the day they left the counseling office. Hearing her talk about not being worthy of love, and never being someone's wife pushed him harder. He wanted to be the one to prove her wrong. Kyle had made up in his mind that he would spend the rest of his life showing her just how worthy she was.

                              Kyle
stopped at the brown double doors and turned to face her. She was looking around his shoulders, trying to read the letters on the door. Kyle scooted back more so that he was blocking the writing. When she realized what he was doing, she leaned back and crossed her arms over her chest. Her face was frowning slightly. She looked so pretty to him when she was mad. Her eyes would always slant. They would get so low they almost looked closed.

Kyle grabbed her hands and looked down at her. "You ready?"

"Ready for what?"

"To be my wife?"

"I wouldn't have said yes if I wasn't."

"Well let's do it." Kyle stepped to the side and revealed the front door of the chapel.

He'd text the chaplain after she'd said yes and informed his of his plans. When he readily agreed to marry them, Kyle wasted no time getting to the hospital. He needed to do this now. He didn't want to wait and run the risk of her changing her mind while he was away. He had been nervous the entire walk there, but the gleam coming from her smiling face assured him he'd made the right decision. She kissed him so hard and quick he hadn't even seen it coming. He pushed her backwards off him, grabbing onto both of her hands.

"Whoa girl. Calm down, save some of that for after we say *I do*."

She smiled and waited for him to open the door. Inside, there was already four other people there. There was a man and his wife sitting on the front row, the chaplain, and a woman in the back pew praying. Lay-Lay stood to the side, waiting for him to lead the way. He ushered her to the front, where the Chaplain was waiting. Kyle shook Colonel Greene's hand before kissing his wife on the cheek. He pulled Shalaya over next to him so he could introduce her.

"Colonel Greene, this is my Shalaya." Lay-Lay stretched her hand out so she could shake his before doing the same to his wife.

"It's so good to finally meet you. I've heard nothing but great things from Kyle. He's very fond of you, sweetheart. I wish you both nothing but love and happiness," Colonel Greene's wife said.

Kyle had invited them both to witness him and Shalaya's union. Of course, they were overjoyed. Once all introductions had been made, they went to the altar. The Chaplain smiled at them both before he got down to business. The whole thing went pretty fast, only stopping because Shalaya was upset about not having a ring for him. He assured her it was okay, but she was still upset. After promising they'd go look for one immediately after this, they continued. Kyle had set it up to where they got their marriage license and everything done right there once they finished.

"How does it feel to be Mrs. Taylor?" he asked as they walked hand-in-hand to the car.

"Just like I thought it would." Lay-Lay's eyes were misty as he held the door open for her.

He thought about asking what was wrong, but he changed his mind. He figured maybe she was just happy.

Once he was in, he drove straight to the mall, like he'd promised her he would. Inside of Kay Jewelers, Lay-Lay marveled over the beautiful wedding bands. None of them could top hers, but it didn't hurt to look. The men's section wasn't as large as the women's had been, but they had some nice stuff. She looked at all the rings before having Kyle try on her three favorites. The one she chose matched hers the best. It was a diamond-encrusted white gold band with three separate rows of diamonds. It was perfect! The asking price was a little steep, and no matter how much he'd spent on hers, he didn't want her shelling out that kind of cash on him. He tried everything except falling on the floor and throwing a tantrum to get her not to buy it, but she did anyway. As much of a fuss as he'd made, he couldn't say he didn't like it. It was nice, but a little too much for his liking. He would have been just fine with a fifty-dollar ring from Wal-Mart.

"I have one more surprise for you."

"Tell me what it is. I don't like surprises." Kyle thought about it for a minute before deciding to tell her.

"We're flying to my parent's house tomorrow morning. My mom wants to see us."

Lay-Lay stopped in her tracks. "You told your parents?"

"Well, kind of. I told my daddy, and you already know how my mama is. She wouldn't let him rest until he'd told her. She'd happy. She loves you."

"Okay. How long are we staying?"

"For two days, then we're coming back home." She nodded her head and started back walking.

*****

Life was starting to be too much. Smoke sat up in his bed and grabbed the half-smoked blunt and lit it. He looked over his shoulder, careful not to wake Lana. She'd insisted on spending the night last night, and she still hadn't left. Normally he wouldn't have allowed this, but he was lonely. His break up with Lay-Lay was getting the best of him. Had he known not being with her would be this bad, he would have fought harder to keep her. The pain in his heart was foreign. He didn't do this.

Stressing over women was something he'd made it his business not to do. As he let the smoke from his blunt fill his lungs, he thought about all the stuff he'd put her through. It was a lot! It seemed like the more he did, the tighter she held on. Her mouth was sick, but he missed hearing it. Out of all the women he'd been with, she was the most loyal. Of course there was Kristen, but it wasn't the same. He loved Kristen to death, but not even she could compare to what he felt for Lay-Lay.

Lana was nice and he was actually feeling her, but that shit wasn't what he needed either. Her neediness was actually starting to get on his nerves. In the beginning he and Lana were just sex partners, but eventually became more than that. He liked her because she played her position, but these days were different. She was starting to get out of hand. She was so fucking needy, unlike Lay-Lay and Kristen, who handled shit without him having to tell them to. If Lana didn't get her shit together, he would be kicking her ass to the curb soon.

He took another pull from his blunt before looking at Lana again. She was knocked out, and he was glad. He eased out of the bed and grabbed his phone. He walked into the living room, where he sat down on the couch to watch football. He scrolled through his messages before returning the calls of his clients. He had been out of the shop since he'd gotten, shot and it was time to get back to business. He scheduled a few cuts for the day before calling King.

"What's up boy, with your crippled ass."

"Shit, my nigga. What's going on?" Smoke asked as he sat up on his sofa

"I'm at the doctor with Jade right now, but I need a cut. When you taking your ass back to work?"

"All right, well come through today around three, I'll be there." Smoke watched Lana walk down the stairs and into the kitchen. He and King stayed on the phone for another few minutes talking before they hung up. Smoke looked at the clock, and it was already one o' clock. If he was going to make it to work any time today, he had to get started now. Since he'd been shot, he was moving a little slower due to the pain in his stomach. He was almost up the stairs when he heard Lana behind him.

"You going to work today?"

"Yeah."

Lana massaged Smoke's shoulders. "I don't want you to. You should stay here with me. I'm off today."

Smoke's face frowned before he shook his head. If that's what she thought he was about to do, she had lost her mind. That was definitely not happening. The only thing he was doing today was going to check on Kristen and his kids, then heading to work.

"Lana, I got to work. What the fuck are you thinking about?" She stood in front of him twirling her thumbs.

"I just wanted to spend some time with you. I have to go out of town tomorrow to see my parents, and I wanted to be with you for a little while before then." This was news to Smoke. He had no idea she was doing any of that. *Thank God!* he thought as he entered the shower.

"It's all good. I'll just see you when you get back." He waited for an answer from her, but heard nothing.

Obviously she wasn't feeling his answer, but he didn't care. The saying that *the grass isn't always greener on the other side* was proving to be true. He'd contemplated leaving Lay-Lay a few times in the past for her, and for the life of him he couldn't figure out why. Maybe it was because she was only fun when he wasn't supposed to be dealing with her. Now that he could have her any time he wanted to, he didn't want her. Every time he looked up, Lana was in his ear on some bullshit.

She wasn't cut out for the main chick role in his life. She was better at being the side bitch. Smoke finished showering and got out. When he got into the bedroom, she was getting dressed. He didn't bother to acknowledge her, because he wanted her to leave. If he said anything concerning her clothing, she might decide to stay. When he was satisfied with his attire, he grabbed his keys and left. It didn't take long for him to reach Kristen's house, because she lived right around the corner from him.

He'd made sure that when he moved her into her new spot that she was close to him. By no means did he want to live with her, but he wanted to be close to his shorties. His kids were his life. He loved Caleb, and their newest addition Cailyn. They'd found out last week that Kristen was having a girl. When he pulled into the driveway, he saw her car parked outside, along with another one.

He didn't know who it was, so he didn't want to overreact. He knew Kristen had more sense than to let a nigga lay up in the spot he was paying the bills at, but he still didn't trust her. When he got to the door, he used his key and walked in. She and her sister were sitting on the couch watching TV. She tried to get up when she saw him come in, but her growing stomach got the best of her.

"Sit back down girl, I'll come to you," Smoke nodded his head at her sister as she grabbed her things to leave. Once he locked the door behind her, he sat down next to Kristen. "How you feeling today?"

"I'm fine. Just a little tired. What about you? Your stomach feeling better?" Smoke lay back and put his head on her thigh.

"Yeah I'm good. You hungry?"

"Nah I just cooked. You want me to fix you a plate?"

Smoke hadn't even thought about food until she mentioned it. He told her yeah and sat up so she could move. He stood up so he could help her from the sofa. When she was flat on her feet, they were only inches apart, due to the bulge in her belly. Her hands were still in his as he stared at her face.

"What? Why you looking at me like that?"

"Nothing baby girl, pregnancy looks good on you." He kissed her forehead before stepping out of her way. She smiled and headed for the kitchen. The black biker shorts she wore showcased her round ass, making his dick hard. Against his better judgment, he followed her into the kitchen. She was leaning over the counter fixing his food. Smoke walked behind her and pressed his body against hers, being careful not to hurt her stomach. His hands roamed up to her full breast and massaged her nipples through the thin shirt she wore.

"You always feel so good to me," he said into her ear. She'd sat his plate down, and now had her hands resting on the counter top. She moaned as he slid his hand down the front of her shorts and massaged her dripping wet pearl. That was one of the best things about Kristen when she was pregnant. She was always wet and ready. He rubbed faster when he heard her moan his name. "You want me to stop?" She shook her head no before laying it back and resting it against his shoulder. Smoke took this opportunity to lick on her neck. He bit down on the soft skin just below her ear.

Kristen was now pressing her body backwards against him. Before he could continue his rendezvous with her neck, she turned around to face him. Her mouth was on his within seconds. Smoke pressed his hard on against her thigh so she could feel how ready he was. Kristen whimpered with need as he picked her up and placed her gently on the counter. He was busy pushing the food containers out of the way while she sucked on his bottom lip. Her hands fumbled with the drawstrings on his pants as she tried to release his baby maker.

"Just chill baby. Daddy got you." Kristen's mood dwindled with that one comment. She scooted back and removed his hands from her body.

"Smoke, we can't do this."

"What you mean we can't do this? Yes the fuck we can. You're my baby mama I'ma always have rights to the pussy." Smoke didn't know what Kristen's problem was, but she had better fix it. His dick was hard, and she was the reason for it.

"That's the problem. I'm more than just a baby mama, Smoke. I deserve happiness. I want to be with a man that loves me for who I am, and not because I have his kids, or just because his main bitch doesn't want him anymore. I'm not with this shit anymore. You should leave." Kristen looked at the floor before looking at him.

Smoke stood dumbfounded as she hopped down off the counter top and continued fixing his food. Once she was finished, she placed the Tupperware top over it and went to the refrigerator to get him a soda. Smoke watched her scurry around the kitchen gathering napkins, eating utensils, and a bag to put it in. He couldn't believe she'd shut him down like that. There had never been a time where Kristen denied him, and she had him at a loss for words. When she was done, she stopped in front of him and grabbed his hand.

"Come on. I'll walk you to the door." He followed quietly. She was about to open the door when he stopped her.

"Kris, I love you. I really do and I understand why you stopped me. You do deserve the best baby girl." He kissed her forehead and proceeded out of the door.

Kristen watched Smoke leave and wanted to fall on the ground kicking and screaming. She loved him with her entire heart. She just wished he could see it. She would bend over backwards and do splits five months pregnant if that meant he would choose to be with her. She was no fool; as much as he tried to play it cool, he was hurting over Lay-Lay. Hell, what person wouldn't be down about a relationship he'd been in forever?

Kristen could relate to the heartbreak because she'd experienced it on many occasions because of him. He and her had been together long before Lay-Lay came along, but you couldn't tell by the way he treated her. He had kicked her straight to the curb once he'd started kicking it with Lay-Lay. Kristen knew she was playing herself all the times she kept messing around with him while he was with Lay, but that was over now. Seeing the state Lay-Lay was in the day she shot at them opened her eyes. Smoke was a good nigga, but he wasn't ready to do right. Whenever they were together, she could feel the love he had for her, but if it was the same kind he gave

Lay-Lay she didn't want it.

Smoke had run that damn girl crazy. On most days, Kristen felt sorry for helping him dog Lay-Lay, but it wasn't intentional. She loved Smoke just as much as Lay did, and she was entitled to his love just as she was, if not more being that she had him first. I guess there's something about bullets flying in your direction that gives you a change of heart. She loved Smoke, and would be the first person to take him–back once he was ready to do right. Many people might call her stupid but they'd never understand. She'd carried two kids for this man, and would have him ten more if he asked. All she wanted was love and loyalty, and she'd give Smoke the world.

"Just do right Smoke, damn," she said out loud as she watched his truck back out of her driveway.

Kristen felt her stomach jump. She looked down, and her daughter was kicking all over the place. With her hand over her stomach, she headed towards Caleb's room. He was taking a nap, so she decided to start on Cailyn's baby book. The pictures she pasted inside of she and Smoke made her cry, but she wouldn't give in this time. If he didn't get his shit together, she was moving on. She had to find her kids an everyday daddy. They deserved a two-parent home, whether it was with Smoke or not.

Chapter 2

The gold walls and black chairs in Smoke'sshop made the whole building pop. Each chair was occupied, including some of the ones in the waiting area. It was jumping as usual, and he was happy to be back. He had been bored cooped up in the house with Lana's ass since he'd been out of the hospital, and it felt good to be around some of his boys. They all greeted him with laughter and jokes as he made his way to his booth. Being the owner of his own barbershop chain had its perks.

He'd been out for a few days, and had still been making money. It was almost like the dope game, just better since there were no risks of going to jail. He had just cleaned his chair when he heard a pair of familiar voices. When he looked up, King and Dallas were coming through the door. They dapped the men up as they made their way to the back. It was no secret that they used to run the streets. Everybody knew and respected the three of them.

"They letting handicaps cut hair now?" Dallas joked as he slapped hands with Smoke.

"Hell yeah nigga, you ain't know? They can't keep a real nigga down," King dapped Smoke up and sat in his chair. "What y'all niggas doing today?"

"Shit. I just left the doctor with Jade, checking on my lil one. I scooped this nigga up when I dropped her off with Morgan. His head nappy as shit, so make sure you get him next."

"Bruh yo shit looking just as bad as mine. It's this nigga fault. If he could keep his dick to himself, we could get cuts on the regular. Got women trying to kill his ass." They all burst out laughing.

"Y'all niggas think that shit is funny, Lay fucked my ass up."

"Smoke, you must have forgot we were there? She threatened my ass too," King said.

Smoke's mood dropped. "I miss her ass though, real shit. I ain't know it would be like this."

King and Dallas shared a similar smirk as they tried to hold in their laugh. They already knew Smoke was going to start feeling it sooner or later. They'd both been there with Jade and Morgan in the past, and they knew how it felt. Smoke stood silent, waiting for one of them to say something, but neither of them did.

"Ain't no sunshine when she's gone, only darkness every day. Ain't no sunshine when she's gone and this house just ain't no home anytime that she goes away," King sang loudly. He caught everybody's attention as soon as he began. Everybody in the barbershop had turned around and was looking at them. It didn't help that King could sing like hell too. To say Smoke was embarrassed would be an understatement. To add insult to injury, Dallas had pulled out his phone and started playing the real song by Bill Withers. The entire shop was laughing and making jokes.

"Bruh y'all lame as hell for that shit," Smoke said as he laughed.

"Nah nigga, you lame as hell for thinking we're going to feel sorry for your ass. How many times did we tell you to get your shit together?" King reminded him.

"King, on top of us telling his ass, he was right there when Morgan and Jade was taking our asses through the ringer. Women do the fucking most, bruh. If you knew Lay-Lay was who you wanted, you should have sat your ass down." Smoke understood everything King and Dallas were saying, but it didn't ease the pain.

"Y'all know she up there living with that nigga?" Smoke watched King and Dallas look at each other before laughing again. King nodded his head yeah. Dallas started talking.

"Yeah, Morgan told me. I'm sorry about that shit, man. I know that's hard."

"She just left my ass and went straight to that nigga too. She had to have been fucking around with him while we were together."

"From my understanding, they've been feeling each other for a while but never took it there. They just had sex not too long ago for the first time." King turned in his seat so he could see Smoke's face when he said the last part. Smoke tried to hide the sick feeling in his stomach, but failed miserably. He couldn't think about

Lay-Lay giving her goods to another nigga. That thought alone nearly brought him to tears.

"Dude, I know your ass ain't about to cry?" Dallas asked once he saw the look on Smoke's face.

"Look Smoke, we just fucking with you man. We're trying to make light of this fucked up situation. Take it from me, it gets easier. You just got to man up and take this shit. You saw how crazy the gotdamn girl was acting? You drove Lay-Lay insane. Y'all can't be together like that. It hurts, but all I can say is get you somebody new and try to numb the pain," Dallas said.

"What about Kristen, or that nurse?" King asked.

Smoke went on to tell his friends about both women, making sure to include everything. He even went as far as to let them know how Kristen had acted this morning. They were shocked about that one. Even after they'd finished getting their haircuts, King and Dallas chilled at the barbershop for a while. Smoke knew they were trying to keep his mind of his situation, so he welcomed the company. By the time it was time for the shop to close, Smoke had made up his mind. His boys were right; he had to move on. He and Lay-Lay's relationship was poisonous. Maybe it was better for them to love one another from a distance.

*****

"Jesus loves me this I know, for the bible tells me so," Kristen sang to Caleb and Cailyn.

She had just gotten Caleb into bed and was singing him to sleep as she did every night. She spent the entire day cleaning her house, and she was tired. Anytime she sang, her baby girl would kick around to let her know she was listening too. Caleb's eyes had closed, and she could hear him snoring lightly so she got up to leave. She left his door cracked and went into her bedroom to take a shower.

Once she'd stripped down and turned the water on, she heard her front door close. This let her know that Smoke was there. He was the only other person that had a key. Not even her sister had one, and she liked it that way. Kristen was a private person, and didn't like any and everybody around her kids. She proceeded into the shower after hearing the familiar cling of his keys. She grabbed her shampoo and began to lather it in her hair.

"What you doing, Kris? Let me do that," Smoke said as she watched him undress.

"I'm only washing my hair, Smoke."

"My grandma told me if you put your hands above your head you could wrap the cord around the baby's neck. If you strangle my daughter, I'ma strangle your little ass."

Kristen smiled as she listened to him talk about their second child. She loved how caring he was with their kids. She stood back some so he had room enough to join her. Once his whole body was in, he finished washing her hair.

"How was work?"

"It was cool. It felt good to be back. I ain't even know I missed being around them niggas like that. King and Dallas stopped by for a few hours."

"Well that's good. I'm glad you're feeling better," Kristen said as she stepped around him to rinse her hair. She could feel him looking at her, but she wasn't about to be the one to address the elephant in the room. He'd brought it up, so he'd be the one to acknowledge it.

"Kris, I've been thinking a lot about what you said earlier. You were right, you do deserve better." She didn't say anything; she wanted to let him finish. She'd already known she was right. "I've been thinking maybe we should give us a try."

"Come again?"

"I think we should try being in a relationship."

"Are you fucking kidding me right now, Jaylen? You're only saying that shit because Lay-Lay doesn't want your ass any more. I'm not a *win by default* kind of girl. You can have that, because I ain't feeling it." Kristen was seething with anger. Initially, she'd thought she would be okay with him choosing her second, but she wasn't; that only pissed her off. Smoke could take that mess somewhere else.

"Kristen, chill out with all that hot shit. I'm trying to give us a shot for our kids, not because you're finally standing up for yourself. I could care less about that shit. If you want to try with me then say so, if not then say that shit too, but don't sit her popping slick like I'm some kind of lame, because I will slap the shit out of you"

"Nigga please," Kristen said as she shut the water off and got out.

She was in her bedroom getting dressed when she heard the water come back on. He stayed in there until she'd laid down and was about to go to sleep. When he emerged completely naked and wet, Kristen had to hold her legs together. He was making her want him in the worst way right now. *He knows what he's doing.* He went into the closet and came back out in a pair of briefs. He'd made sure to keep him a stock of clothing there for when he stayed over.

"Lock the door on your way out."

"Kristen, shut up talking to me and take your ass to sleep." Kristen snickered at the pissy mood he was in.

"Don't get mad with me because I called you on your shit."

"Go to fucking bed, stupid ass girl," Smoke said as he walked around to the other side of the bed and got in. He made sure to pull all of the covers off her. Kristen laughed as she sat straight up in the bed.

"Smoke, why you playing games? It's too late for this."

Instead of answering her, he let go of some of the covers so she could have some. When she laid back down, he pulled her into his arms so that her head was on his chest.

"Goodnight Jaylen." His body stiffened for a moment before he replied. Smoke lay away, thinking about he and Lay-Lay. When Kristen had called him Jaylen, it took his mind back to Shalaya. She was the only woman that ever really called him that. It didn't sound as good coming from Kristen's mouth as it did hers. He became teary-eyed as he thought about her living and sleeping with another man. Smoke didn't know if it was the fact that she was with someone else, or that he knew she was happy without him. Either way it went, it hurt. A lone tear slipped down his cheek. He was missing the hell out Lay-Lay right now. Not even lying in bed with Kristen could ease it.

*****

The cold air brushed harshly against Lay-Lay's face as she and Kyle made their way to the front of his parents' home. The Christmas lights that adorned the outside of the house instantly warmed Lay-Lay's heart. She loved Christmas time, and before she'd gotten here, she hadn't really thought about it. She'd seen a few houses decorated, but she still hadn't paid it any mind until now.   Christmas this year would definitely be one for the books. She had her husband, and that alone was enough to make it a great day. The front door of the massive brick home opened, and Hannah stood there smiling. She waved her arms and motioned for them to come inside. Kyle pulled Lay along the sidewalk and up the stairs. He had grabbed her hand the moment they were out of the car, as he always did. As soon as they were inside of the house, Hannah grabbed them in a big hug.

"I'm so happy that you all made it," she beamed.

"I am too Ma, where's Dad?"

"He's in the den watching TV, you two go ahead and put your things away, and then we'll go see him."

Kyle and Lay-Lay headed towards the back, where his old room was located. It was still decorated the same, with all of his Army posters and pictures on the wall. The only thing that was different was the covers on the bed. Lay-Lay remembered everything about this room. She'd snuck in there every chance she got when she was there visiting during the summers. Kyle sat their bags in the corner before closing the door. He sat down on the bed and leaned back on his elbows.

"Come here," Kyle motioned her over with his finger. Lay-Lay shook her head no.

"Not in your parents' house. It's not happening."

"I just want a kiss." The grin on his face let her know he was lying, but she went anyway. She leaned down on top of him gently before placing her mouth on his. He gripped her butt and pulled her all the way down on top of him.

"Ummm, boy you just don't know how wet you keep your girl."

"Let me see for myself."

"Maybe later handsome, but you know like I do that Hannah is out there waiting on us."

Kyle laughed as she slid slowly off his body. When she was eye level with his stomach, she raised his shirt and licked his rock hard abs. She circled the deep cut lines along his side with her tongue, and kissed them before standing back up.

"Now why you do that shit?"

"Because you're looking good enough to eat," she winked and proceeded out of the door. She was sure he needed a minute to get himself together after that. When she walked into the living room, Mr. Arlington was sitting in his favorite recliner watching the football game. As soon as he saw her, he smiled and got up for a hug.

"There's my little firecracker," he embraced her in a fatherly hug. "I missed my girl. How you been, sweetheart?"

"You want the truth or a lie?" He gave her a knowing look before she chuckled. She had always loved her relationship with Mr. Arlington. He was like the father she'd never had. "Well I'm sure Kyle has filled you in on my foolishness, so I'll just tell you I'm doing a lot better now, thanks to him."

"Shalaya, you know I love you sweetheart. Any time you need to talk, give me a call. I'm never too busy to help one of my babies." Lay-Lay was too busy crying to acknowledge what he'd just said. She had longed for a father her entire life, and she'd finally gotten one. Upon noticing her tears, he was out of his recliner and next to her within seconds. "Everything's fine firecracker, we all have our moments where this old life just beats us down, but that's okay. As long as you come back up swinging, you'll win every time."

"Back off my woman, old man." Kyle was standing in the doorway. Arlington laughed as he kissed Lay-Lay's cheek before standing to embrace his son. They grabbed each other in a tight hug, while making jokes on one another. Kyle looked over at Lay-Lay. "You alright bae?"

"Yeah I'm fine. I'm about to go see if Ms. Hannah needs help with anything." She was about to walk past when Kyle reached his arm out and stopped her. She looked up into his handsome face, waiting for him to say something. No words came; instead, it was his lips. They pressed to the side of her head before moving so she could keep going. She roamed the house until she found her place in the kitchen with Hannah. She was standing at the stove cooking, so Lay-Lay took a seat at the bar.

"I've heard about what's been going on. What's the matter with you, Shalaya? Don't you know you can't put that much stock into a man? I got the mind to slap you for doing something that crazy. Don't you ever in your life give a man that much power over you again."

"I know Ms. Hannah, but he just kept playing with my emotions. I didn't know I was in that deep until I had the gun pointed at my head. You don't understand; I bent over backwards doing whatever I could for him, and he still found time to cheat. Mr. Arty has probably never taken you through anything like the mess I've been through with Smoke."

"First things first, call me mama," Hannah smiled at her before continuing. "Now that that's out of the way, let me school you real quick. You aren't the first woman to be cheated on and lied to. Furthermore, you won't be the last. When you took him back after the first time he cheated, you asked for any heartache that came after that. You should have kicked him to the curb right then. Once he saw that you would allow his doggish ways, of course he was going to continue. What man wouldn't? I know it hurts baby, I know it does, but you have to be stronger than that. If there's one thing I hate more than a sorry man, it's a weak woman. Shalaya, you're far from weak, so act like it. You're a young educated queen that's got plenty of business about yourself. Don't you ever in your life let a man treat you less than what you're worth. I don't care who you're involved with, you love yourself first. I was in love with someone else before I met Arty, and he did me bad. I didn't know if I was going or coming most days, but I chose to leave. I couldn't spend the rest of my life dealing with that. When God sent me Arlington, I was the happiest woman on the planet. He treated me the way a man should treat a woman. I made sure to teach Morgan her worth early in life so she didn't make the same mistakes as I did. Arlington and I have raised Kyle right; he's everything a man should be. You're safe with him. Do you hear me, little girl? "

"Yes ma'am, I do. Thank you."

"Don't thank me with your mouth, thank me with your actions." Lay-Lay nodded her head, letting her know she understood. "Now on to a brighter note. You don't know how happy I was when Arty told me you two were married. It made my day to know my son had someone to love him just as hard as he would love her. Kyle's a sweet and gentle man. When he loves, it's limitless and real. You've got yourself an amazing husband in him, baby." Lay-Lay's smile could have lit up the kitchen when she thought of Kyle.

"Mama, I love him so much. You did your thing with him, and I thank God for him daily. Never in my life did I think I would deserve, let alone find and marry a man of his caliber. Kyle's the sweetest love I've ever known, and each day with him is like a gift. I'ma love him forever, mama. I don't even want to get started on how fine he is. Whew Lord, your son is fine."

"Girl, I know my baby fine. Just like his daddy."

Lay-Lay and Hannah high fived each other as they thought of their husbands. Before long, Lay-Lay and Hannah had cooked up the entire kitchen and had dinner ready and waiting. When they all sat down for dinner, Kyle made sure to sit next to Lay. They all dug in and began to eat.

"Hannah, baby you put your foot in this cornbread," Arlington said taking another bite.

"Shalaya made that sweetheart, not me."

"I'm no stranger in the kitchen, Mr. Arty. I've had to cook for my mother and siblings my whole life. My mama hasn't always been the best, so I had to stand in and do what I needed to do."

"You want kids?" Hannah asked.

"I'm actually pretty good on kids right now. Morgan and Jade have enough for me." Lay-Lay purposely brought up Morgan's kids, because she knew how soft they were on them. She was right; the conversation jumped from her directly to Morgan, Dallas, and the babies. She was grateful, because she didn't want anyone planning her future for her, especially not the arrival of her future babies.

The ceiling fan was constantly spinning, keeping the small room cool. Kyle lie awake thinking about his deployment. He needed to tell Shalaya soon. Now just wasn't the time. He'd tell her once they got back home, when they were alone and could have loud make up sex once she was finish being mad.

"You must want some of this good wet stuff?" Lay-Lay asked him as she grabbed a handful of his hard pipe.

"I thought you were sleep."

"I thought you were too until I felt this little guy poking me in my butt."

"Well give him what he want then," Kyle smiled wickedly as he pulled her on top of him. He was tired and he needed to make love to his wife. Being inside of her always cleared his mind. She mounted him, and being that she was already pantyless, he was able to slide right in.

"AHHH SHIT SHALAYA!" he groaned loudly.

"Boy you better be quiet before your parents hear you," Lay-Lay held her finger up to her lips.

Kyle's eyes rolled into the back of his head as he grabbed on to both sides of her hips. He pushed his hips upward off the bed, trying to get as deep in her as he could. She bit her bottom lip as she began to slowly move up and down. Her hair fell down into her face when she leaned her head forward. She looked so fucking sexy with her face distorted in pleasure. He reached up and grabbed both sides of her neck, and pulled her face down so he could kiss her. He tugged on her full lips as he continued to plunge his hips up into her wetness. Fed up with playing the submissive role, he lifted her up and lifted them both off the bed.

"Bend that ass over, Shalaya." He pushed her face down onto the bed and grabbed a hand full of her hair. He slid right back into her moist heat with no problem. "You're always so wet for me." He began sliding in and out of her as she looked at him over her shoulder.

"Harder Kyle. Fuck me harder, baby."

That was all he needed to hear. He picked up his pace and began beating her walls out. Every time he would slam into her, her essence was trickle down his thighs. *Man I love this shit!* Lay-Lay's large, round ass bounced against his thighs relentlessly as he pounded in and out of her. With her hair still wrapped around his hand, he pulled her head backwards so his mouth was next to her ear.

"Cum on my dick, Lay." Her legs instantly began to shake as an orgasm took over her entire body. He watched her bite down onto the silk pillowcase until her body stopped shaking. Kyle leaned down on her back and sucked on the side of her neck until he too felt himself on the edge.

"Come on Kyle. Cum for me baby," she begged.

Not long after, he released his load inside of her. He didn't even bother to pull himself out of her; he just pulled her onto him and rolled backwards onto the bed. She separated them when she turned over and snuggled against his chest. Before long, she was snoring. Kyle kissed the top of her forehead and closed his eyes. Hopefully sleep would find him soon.

Chapter 3

The time they'd spent at his parent's house was well needed. It had given him and Shalaya the reassuring boost that they'd needed for their marriage. They had just gotten back to his house when he heard Lay-Lay's phone ringing. He was about to take it to her when she yelled for him to answer it.

"Dang, y'all answering each other's phones now?" Jade asked.

"Nah, forget all that. I'm trying to figure out why you and Lay-Lay taking trips to Mommy and Daddy's house without telling me. How y'all know we didn't want to come?" Kyle laughed as Morgan and Jade continued firing question after question at him.

"Well hello to you too, ladies. How are you beauties doing this afternoon?"

"Don't try to butter us up, we're fine," Morgan said before he handed the phone off to Lay-Lay.

"Don't y'all two heffas call interrogating my man."

Both women screamed hello in unison. It seemed like forever since the last time all of them had talked. With everything Lay had going on, they'd wanted to give her some time to get herself together. They made sure to call and check in with Kyle every day to check on her. Kyle walked out of the room and went to take a shower.

Just before he got in, his cell phone beeped with a text message. It was from his buddy Jones. He'd invited him and Lay-Lay over for dinner later that night. Kyle shot him a text letting him know they'd be there before headed back into the bathroom. Once he'd showered, he dried off and got straight into bed. Their flight had him wore out. He was sleep as soon as his head hit the pillow.

"Scoot over," he heard Lay-Lay say as she slid in next to him. He wrapped his arm around her as soon as she got in.

"I love you husband."

"I love you too wife."

Kyle scooted closer to her and bit her neck. They slept for a few hours before waking up. He was up before she was, so he went into the closet to find something to wear to Jones' cookout.

"Why you leave?"

"We have somewhere to be, babe. Get up."

"What? Where we going?"

"Jones is having a cookout. He invited us." Kyle watched her throw her head back down onto the pillow.

"Jones is just a regular old party animal, huh? Who all is going to be at this little cookout? I don't have time for a replay of his last little gathering. I can't promise that I won't slap one of your old hoes."

Kyle laughed and pulled her out of the bed. She was stark naked as she moved around the room gathering her things out of her bags.

"When are you going to unpack?"

He had been meaning to ask her that for a while, but it always slipped his mind. In his mind, he assumed she was staying in South Carolina with him–at least until he left on deployment. Lay-Lay shrugged her shoulders as she rummaged through her bag for a pair of panties. "You do know you have to live here with me since you're my wife, right?"

"Of course I know that, Major Taylor. I'll unpack and stuff soon. Maybe later." She got up, kissed his lips, and handed him her clothes to iron. It took them both approximately an hour and a half before they were both ready. Lay-Lay was dressed in all black, minus the red pumps and clutch she carried. She French braided her hair into a long braid going diagonally down the back of her head with minimal make-up.

Kyle matched her with the all black. He chose to keep his simple and rock his red Toro four's and red Phillies fitted hat. They were out of the house and on their way in no time. When they pulled up to Jones' house, there were three other cars there as well. Kyle recognized two of them as Mack's car and their other friend Porter's truck.

He kissed her lips. "Behave."

"I'll think about it," she smiled as he got out to come around and open her door. Hand and hand, they walked to the front door. Kyle rung the bell and waited for the door to open. Jones appeared immediately, carrying a pan of bread.

"Come on in. They party's just getting started." He stepped to the side so they could enter. The place looked totally different from the last time they'd been there. It was clean and not packed. In the great room, Porter, Mack, and two females Kyle had never seen were watching American Sniper. He and Lay-Lay joined them on the sofa after making introductions.

"I like those shoes, girl," the woman with Porter said to Lay-Lay

"Thanks doll. I was just about to say the same thing about that dress. You're killing it! It compliments your skin tone beautifully,"

"Thank you. I got from a mall in Atlanta. They don't have anything up here."

"So you're from Atlanta?"

"Born and raised."

"Girl, me too. I thought I was just being picky when I could never find anything at this mall."

Kyle was happy Lay-Lay and the girl was having such a good time with one another. He knew how guarded his baby could be, but surprisingly she seemed to be stepping out of shell tonight. Ever so often, Kyle would catch Mack's eyes on Lay-Lay, but he just shrugged it off.

Shalaya was a beautiful woman. He couldn't stop every man that was looking at her. Judging by the way the girl was sitting next to him with an attitude, she too had caught him. Kyle smirked as he turned his head. He was wondering why she hadn't joined in on the conversation with the other girls.

"My wife is on her way back with the cakes, we'll eat as soon as she gets here," Jones said as he joined everyone in the living room. Lay was still talking to Porter's girlfriend when his phone rang. The caller ID told him it was Morgan. When he answered, she demanded to speak to Lay-Lay.

"What I dun' told you about calling my man phone?" Lay asked as she stood up to excuse herself. She told Kyle she was going to stand on the porch to talk to Morgan. He nodded his head, but instructed her to go in the bathroom instead since it was cold outside. Jones showed her the bathroom before returning back to everyone else.

****

*

Lay-Lay was still talking to Morgan when she heard a knock at the door.

"Hold on, Morg."

Kyle was standing there smiling. "Come on, Jones' wife is here."

Lay poked her bottom lip out before telling Morgan she'd call her back when she got home. She handed Kyle his phone and followed him down the hall. Being with Kyle was so relaxing. She had never been able to just freely take Smoke's phone without him damn near breaking his neck to take it from her. Kyle had forked his phone over without a second thought. *Thank you Lord for this man.* Lay-Lay wrapped both of her arms around his waist from behind and laid her head on his back. He was so much taller than her, and she loved it.

"Didn't I tell you to behave before got out the car?"

"I just can't control myself when you're around. You sexy body is like a magnet for my hands."

"Man, your ass is crazy girl," Kyle laughed as he led them into the kitchen. Being that she was still holding onto his waist, they had to walk a little slower so they wouldn't trip over each other's feet. When they got into the kitchen, Lay leaned on the counter and pulled Kyle closer to her. He was so big that she was sure no one could see her behind him. If her manicured hands weren't resting on his abs, they probably wouldn't have even known she was behind him.

"Give me a kiss and I'll stop," she said from behind him. He turned around, resting both hands on the counter behind her. He dipped his head low before kissing her waiting lips.

"Damn, Major Taylor. This is one for the books. I've never seen you act like this in public, or private for that matter," Mack said as he watched the public display of affection Lay and Kyle were putting on.

"I ain't never been in love like this before," Kyle said as he turned back around to face his friends.

"Well move so I can see her," Jones' wife said as she walked into the kitchen. Kyle smiled at her as he reached back and pulled Lay-Lay from behind him. "This is Shalaya. Shalaya, this is Jones' wife La–"

"Lana," Lay-Lay finished for him. Lay-Lay's eyes almost popped out of her head. She just knew she had to be seeing things. This was not the same bitch that Smoke had been cheating on her with for who knows how long. The look on Lana's face mirrored hers. She looked like she wanted to piss all over herself.

"You two know each other?" Confusion was evident in Kyle's voice.

"Umm, yeah. I uhh…met here while I was in Atlanta," Lana said just as Jones walked over to them.

"She was one of my nurses when I was at the hospital," Lay-Lay said, going along with her lie. This bitch had some nerve. She had better been glad Lay didn't want to act a fool in front of Kyle's friends and embarrass him, or Ms. Thing would have been put out on front-street ASAP.

"The world is so small. Who would have ever guessed you two's paths would have crossed like this?"

"You're right, Jones. Who would have thought," Lay smiled at Lana as she grabbed Kyle's hand and walked towards the table. Once everyone was seated, Lana had the nerve to bless the food. Lay-Lay was almost too nervous to eat it. She prayed over her and Kyle's food again when Lana finished. This was the same hoe that was cheating on her husband with a drug dealer; she was not about to let her pray over her food and she end up choking.

God probably hadn't heard a word she'd said. *Old sinful heffa!* Lay thought as she looked up and met Lana's gaze. She rolled her eyes as hard as she could before looking back down at her plate. While everyone was praying, Lay had taken her phone out and snapped a picture of Lana. She sent the picture to Smoke with a text that said:

Lay-Lay: Ain't this your bitch?

He text back immediately. Something he never did when they were together

Smoke*: Nah. That's Lana lol*

Lay-Lay: Don't try to be cute nigga

Smoke*: I'm not. But yeah that's her. Where y'all at?*

Lay-Lay: I'm having dinner at her and her husband's house tonight

S*moke: HUSBAND??*

Lay-Lay: Yep! Doesn't feel good to be cheated on does it? Lol! Bye Jaylen!

Smoke*: Tell her I'ma put my foot in her ass*

Lay-Lay: I'll do it for you ☺

Smoke*: That's why you my hitta. Lol. Bye Lay-Lay*

Lay couldn't do anything but laugh at Smoke. That nigga was a serious character. She hadn't talked to him since the day she left the hospital, but she couldn't pass up this opportunity to be messy. He needed to know how it feels to be dogged out and cheated on. How ironic was it that his side bitch was married? *Ha! That's what his ass gets.*

"So Shalaya, how did you and Major Taylor meet?" Porter's girlfriend asked, breaking her from her thoughts. She was a sweet girl, so Lay was more than happy to talk to her. She seemed like a person she would actually consider becoming friends with.

"I've been in love with Kyle since I first saw him. I know that sounds cliché, but it's the truth. His sister is my best friend. I spent a lot of summers at their house while we were in college. We've been friends forever up until recently. We decided to give us a real shot, and it's so perfect," Lay-Lay smiled as she looked over at him.

"Y'all know I'm from the North, and our women aren't that developed. Once I laid eyes on all that southern thickness, I couldn't resist her."

"He's been had a thing for this little PYT ever since," Lay-Lay and Kyle both laughed at how silly they were being.

"Aww, y'all are so cute. I just love how happy you make him. But if you don't mind me asking, what is a PYT?" Porter's girlfriend asked.

Lay looked at her like she was crazy. "You've never heard Michael Jackson's song Pretty Young Thing?" She shook her head no. "Well yeah, Kyle is older than me, that's why I always say that."

"So y'all have basically been together all these years, just not official?" Lana asked. All traces of humor left Lay's face as she turned her head slowly so she could see Lana. She knew this bitch didn't call herself trying to be funny.

"That's not what I said. I *said*, he and I have been in love for a long time, that's not the same thing as being together. I was in a very bad relationship a little while ago that Kyle saved me from. It wasn't until then that we decided to make it official. The man I was dealing with before had a problem keeping his dick out of other people's wives. He would fuck anything that had a behind. Although that was bad enough, that wasn't my problem," Lay turned in her seat so that she was now facing Lana directly. "My problem didn't come in until his women started to forget their place. You see, normally side bitches know their role and they play it well, but not his. I guess they started to feel special and forgot who I was. Once they felt that they had the right to talk to me, I knew it was over. He no longer knew how to keep those pitiful ass excuses for women in their lane. Let me tell you something about myself Lana, I'm a very rowdy person and I didn't have the time or the energy to whoop ass every day. You feel me?" Lay-Lay stared her down, waiting for a response. Lana fidgeted in her seat as she drank a sip of her water.

"I understand exactly what you mean Lay-Lay."

"Call me Shalaya, please," Lay-Lay turned back around in her seat and started back eating.

"I knew I liked you," Porter's girlfriend said as she high-fived Lay-Lay across the table. "Some women just don't know their place. You just like me; I will knock a female right back down to her knees about mine."

After a few more awkward moments, the dinner was back in full swing. Ever so often, Lay-Lay would catch Lana's eyes on her, but she wasn't fazed. This was not the game Lana wanted to play with her. Once everybody had gotten done eating, the men retired to the living room to watch the game while the ladies stayed behind to clean up. Well, at least most of them did. The little rude broad Mack had brought with him followed the men into the living room. That was probably her best bet anyways, because she was not Lay-Lay's cup of tea.

"Lay-Lay, you're a real ass female. I like you," Porter's girlfriend said.

"Thanks boo. I like you too."

"Real is rare these days." Lana's words weren't even out of her mouth good before Lay-Lay was on her.

"Bitch, don't get ran through in this fucking kitchen. I've been trying to be nice all night, but if you keep trying me, I won't hesitate to tap that ass."

"Lay-Lay, please. You up here with Kyle pretending to be something you ain't. I know you. Hoe, you ain't no different than me."

Lay rounded the counter top and was in Lana's face within seconds. "Don't ever in your little side bitch life come out the side of you neck to me like that again. You and I are on two different levels. You chasing after my leftovers bitch, get your fucking life before I get it for you." Lay-Lay stood in Lana's face, daring her to say anything.

"Lay-Lay, I knew when we were at the table that you was talking about this scandalous ass bitch. I could see through her fake ass the first time I ever met her," Porter's girlfriend said.

Lana opened her mouth to speak, but Lay-Lay had grabbed her by the neck before she could say anything. She was fed up with Lana. She owed her an ass whooping anyway. Lays fist connected with the side of Lana's face at the same time she slammed her head into the cabinet. Lana looked like she wanted to scream, but she didn't. Satisfied, Lay stepped back and left the kitchen. This was the exact reason she couldn't be with Smoke. She was dealing with his shit and he wasn't even there.

"Baby I'm ready to go."

"All right. You okay?" Kyle asked as he noticed the distressed look on her face.

"Yeah I'm good, let's just go. It was nice to meet you all," Lay-Lay waved as Kyle headed towards her. They said their goodbyes before heading to his truck. They were almost out of the driveway when Porter's girlfriend ran out, waving for them to stop.

"Here's my number, girl. Let's hang out sometimes."

"Okay girl. We sure will," Lay said as she took her card and rolled up the window.

"Everything alright? Did something happen back there?"

"If I tell you something, you have to promise not to tell." Kyle promised before she continued. "Jones' wife Lana, she's sleeping around with Smoke. They've been messing around for months now. She's the one who called the police on me for stabbing Smoke that day."

"Are you serious, Shalaya?"

"Yep. Why do you think I went so hard on her at the table? She was trying to be funny instead of thanking me for not exposing her ass."

"I can't believe this. Jones sent her down there to work and she's been cheating on that nigga the whole time?" Kyle looked disgusted.

"Yeah. I punched her in the kitchen. That's why I left. I'm trying to change and she just brought me right back to where I didn't want to be."

Kyle looked over at Lay and grabbed her hand. He kissed it before resting it on his leg. They held hands all the way back to home.

Chapter 4

The next morning, Kyle was sitting in the living room, trying to put up the Christmas Tree Lay-Lay had made him buy the night before when the doorbell rang. He was hesitant at first, because he wasn't expecting anyone. On top of that, Lay wasn't wearing anything but his tank top while she made them breakfast. When he looked out the peephole, he saw it was Jones.

"Bae, Jones is at the door,"

"Okay," she said as she headed up the stairs to change. By the time she came back, they were sitting in the living room. She waved and kept it moving to the kitchen.

"Sorry for barging in like this so early. I just didn't know where else to go. Lana and I had a fight last night and she left."

"Where'd she go?" Kyle asked as he noticed Lay-Lay peeping around the corner. She mouthed *I told you* before ducking her head back into the kitchen. He hated to see his friend like this. His eyes were red, and he looked like he'd been drinking.

"She said she was going back to Atlanta. I told her that we were deploying next week and she went off, screaming about me not having time for her, and I might die and shit. I don't need this right before we go, man. I can't go over there with my head messed up like this."

Kyle's stomach tightened as soon as the word deployment left Jones' mouth. He knew Lay-Lay was eavesdropping, which meant she'd heard it as well. Not even a whole minute later, she came around the corner with the dishtowel in her hand.

"What deployment?" Jones looked from Kyle to Lay-Lay with wild eyes.

"You didn't tell her? Ah man, I'm sorry sir. I didn't know," he said.

"It's alright man, just go wash up and get some rest. I'll grab you a change of clothes; you can stay here until you sober up. You shouldn't be driving like this," Kyle said as he walked past Lay and up to his room. He needed a few minutes to get his thoughts together. Too bad that wasn't about to happen.

"You're deploying again, Kyle? Why didn't you tell me?"

"Yes. Next week. I didn't tell you because I've been trying to find the right time."

"What? All this time we've been together you could have been told me!"

"I know I should have. I just didn't want you to worry."

"Oh shut up! You knew I would worry anyway. That just comes with the territory. What am I supposed to do if something happens and you don't make it back?" Tears were now sliding down her cheeks non-stop. Kyle crossed the room and held her in his arms.

"If something happens and I don't make it back, you'll be fine. I made sure of that. I had my father switch all of my affairs over to you. You're my wife. You'll get anything that I own, plus more." Lay-Lay sobbed louder before snatching away from him. She looked angry.

"Is that why you married me? OH MY GOSH, YOU MARRIED ME JUST IN CASE YOU DIE? I can't believe you!" Lay-Lay fell into a heap on the floor. She gasped for air as she held on tightly to her chest.

"Shalaya, calm down before you have a panic attack. That's not why I married you, baby. I married you because I love you. I wanted you to be my wife, Shalaya. I was tired of waiting on you to choose me. I married you because I wanted you all to myself. I would never marry you just because I'm deploying!"

"Yes you did, Kyle. You're trying to make me a widow. You want me to stay here and cry myself to death." Lay-Lay grabbed onto his shirt and pulled at it as tears and snot ran down her face. "I don't want to be here without you! You can't go! You have to stay here with me—please baby, please! We just started, it can't be over yet!" Lay-Lay was a mess. The only time he'd seen her this distraught was when she was about to kill herself, and even then she wasn't this upset. She was calmer, like she didn't care. Right now, she was hysterical and inconsolable. Kyle grabbed a hold of her when she started gasping for air again, and shook her lightly.

"Shalaya, listen to me. I am not going to die. Do you hear me? I'm good at my job; I promise I'm coming home. All the other times I deployed, I didn't have a reason to come home, now I do! You're my reason, Shalaya. I'll do whatever it takes to make it back to you baby, okay? You just have to be strong. I can't leave and focus on my job if I'm not sure if you're okay. You have to stay here and hold us down, baby. You're strong. You can do this."

It broke his heart to see her falling apart like this. This was one of his main reasons for not telling her. She got sad every time he left. This time, since they were actually together, she was taking it a lot harder. Kyle ran to the top of the stairs and threw Jones some clothes over the balcony before telling him to use the shower and bed in the spare bedroom. When he returned to his room, he closed and locked the door before stripping completely naked. He undressed Lay-Lay next with no help.

Her entire body was limp, and she looked dazed. He grabbed her from the floor and carried her to the bathroom. Once the shower was hot enough, he stepped in and slid down to the floor. Shalaya lay between his legs, sobbing lightly into his chest as the water cascaded over them. He rubbed his hand up and down her back, trying to soothe her.

"I'm coming home, Shalaya. I promise I'm coming back to you."

"I don't want you to go."

"I know you don't, but I have to. They need me."

"I need you."

Kyle was quiet as he thought about the possibility of him not making it back. Every time they went, there was a risk of dying, but he surely wouldn't tell her that.

"Shalaya, I married you because I love you. I love you so much. I wanted you to always be straight. If I was to die over there, I don't want you to ever want for anything. I put you in this position so that you'll be better off, no matter the situation. I know you can take care of yourself, but I want to take care of you. In life or death, I want to be the one person you can count on. Don't ever think I married you just because I thought I might die, because that's not it." Lay-Lay lie still, looking at the tile. She had stopped crying, but her breathing was still ragged.

"Thank you," she said quietly before turning around and kissing his chest. She straddled his thighs and began licking all over his chest. Her tongue circled his nipples before trailing down his abs and landing on his girth. It sprang to life the moment her lips touched it. She kissed around his thighs before licking up and down his length. He flexed slightly when she took him into her mouth. The amount of pleasure he got from this woman was immeasurable. He had the perfect view of her round ass as she bobbed up and down on his dick. He grabbed the back of her head and guided her head up and down on him.

"DAMN BAE!" he hissed before pulling her head up to his. His tongue was so far down her throat that he was surprised he didn't choke her. "Come give me some," he said, pulling her onto his lap. He relished the feeling of her soft, tight insides as she slid down onto him. She rode him slow and sensual as tears began falling again. Kyle held onto her as tight as he could without stopping her movements. With his head buried deep in her chest, he too shed a few tears. Never in his entire career had leaving been this hard. This woman was his everything. Hearing her cry made his heartache, but this was his life. She cried and rode them both into pure ecstasy.

After their shower, he could tell she felt better. It was still bothering her, but she was functioning. She'd finished cooking breakfast and served him and Jones. Kyle watched her move around the kitchen in a pair of tights and a racer back top. Her wet red hair had air-dried, and it looked beautiful on her. It was big and wavy and framed her face perfectly. She fixed a plate for herself and joined the men in the living room. She sat so close to Kyle that she was able to tuck her feet beneath his thigh. He looked over her and watched her eat.

"What?"

"Nothing. I think you're beautiful."

"Boy please. I know my hair is all over my head right now."

"It is, but it looks good. You look so natural."

"It really does look nice like that, Shalaya," Jones said as he gave a weak smile.

"Thanks y'all." Kyle liked the smile that was returning to her face. He turned his attention back to Jones and instantly felt bad. He wanted to tell him about Lana so bad, but that wasn't his place. He was sitting on the sofa looking like he had been through hell and back. His eyes were still bloodshot red, probably a mix between the liquor and crying. His clothes were too big, being that they were Kyle's, and his head was in desperate need of a cut.

"Jones are you alright?" Lay-Lay asked.

"I'm as good as can be expected."

"It'll get better soon,"

"No it won't. She's been giving me a hard time for a while now. It's like no matter what I do for her it's never enough. I just don't understand. We used to be so good together, but now all she does is complain. She tries to make it about my job, but I've been in the Army since we met. The problem didn't come in until she got that job in Atlanta. I thought it was a good idea then, because I deployed so much and she had family there, but now I'm regretting it. You're a woman Shalaya, you know what she's going through more than I do. Please tell me what's wrong, because I don't know." Kyle looked at Lay and pleaded with his eyes for her not to say anything, but he already knew that was a lost cause. She'd sat her plate down and scooted up to the edge of the sofa.

"Jones listen, if you know you're doing all you can and it's still not good enough for her, then maybe it's time for you to let go. Some women are ungrateful. They don't know a good man when they see one. Take it from me, leave her alone. The heartache isn't worth it. I've been where you're at. Just let it go."

"I don't know if I can."

"Yes you can. It'll be hard at first, but you'll be fine. Use this deployment as time to clear you head. Go over there, help save some lives, and bring your single ass back home." Jones laughed when she said that part. Kyle breathed a little easier now that she hadn't said anything. The last thing Jones needed was this on his brain before going into a war zone.

"You're my new homie, Shalaya. I appreciate a female that can be real with a nigga. Sir, make sure you keep this one on your team."

"This my girl for life right here. Her ass is stuck with me." Kyle said, holding Shalaya's hand up for him to see her ring. Jones' eyes bulged in shock.

"Congratulations sir. I had no idea. That's big right there."

Lay-Lay smiled as she stood to gather their dishes. Once she had all three plates, she left to clean the kitchen. She had only been in there for about ten minutes before Jones announced he was leaving. Kyle was walking him to the door when Lay-Lay stuck her head back around the corner.

"Jones, get your shit together. Don't take your butt over there thinking about Lana and let Kyle get hurt. Trust and believe, I will beat your ass when you get back." Jones laughed so hard it made Kyle feel better. He looked to be in better spirits, which was a good sign.

*****

Christmas music sounded through the house as Lay-Lay baked sugar cookies and hung decorations. She was finally in the spirit enough to stop procrastinating. After Jones had left, she and Kyle went to Wal-Mart and Hobby Lobby to get everything she needed. She felt like a kid running through the aisles. Before going in, Kyle assured her that she could get whatever she wanted and that's what she did. From outside decorations to wrapping paper, she didn't miss a beat. She'd even gone as far as to make Kyle buy a ladder to help with the things she wanted to do outside.

While she sat on the floor lining the dining room table with fake snow, Kyle wrapped the garland around the railing on the staircase. He hadn't wanted to do it, but when she bribed him with kisses and cheesecake for dessert, he began moving faster than she was. As she hummed along with Otis Redding's *Merry Christmas Baby*, Kyle joined her in the living room. She had just stood up to get the boxes with her Christmas people in it when Kyle grabbed her hands and pulled her around in a circle. He was spinning and twirling her all over the living room singing. It didn't take her long to get with the beat before she was dancing right along with him. They danced the whole song with Kyle singing to her.

"I feel like I'm in Paradise," he sang loudly as he kissed her forehead. "I love you baby, for everything that you give me!" He pulled her beneath the mistletoe and dipped her for a kiss. He didn't let her go until the song went off.

"Baby you're so silly," Lay-Lay said as she went back to decorating.

"You like it."

"Of course I do."

"You have my house looking like a circus right now. You know that?" Lay-Lay slapped his arm as she circled the tree with lights.

"It does not. It looks beautiful."

"The only thing in this house that's beautiful is you."

"Look at you trying to spit game. That's cute, Major Taylor," Kyle laughed as he handed the lights back around to her. "Can you go take those cookies out the oven please?" Kyle left with no problem. Lay-Lay laughed, because it was clear that he had no intentions of helping. Her bribe had worn thin, and he was letting it show. When he came back, he had a handful of cookies and a cup of milk.

"You are so sloppy. Why didn't you just put the cookies on a plate?" Kyle shrugged his shoulders before taking a seat on the couch. Once Lay finally finished with the tree, she snuggled under him and turned on her favorite movie, *This Christmas*.

"What day do you leave?"

"Next Wednesday. You staying here while I'm gone?" That question made her pause. She hadn't even given that any thought. She still had her apartment back home, so that's probably where she would go. It wasn't like she knew anybody up here, or had a job for that matter. There was no real reason to stay.

"I'm going home."

"Your home is with me."

"Well you're leaving, so I'm going back to Atlanta. I'll move here fully when you get back." She could feel Kyle shift beneath her. She thought it would be quick, but he kept fidgeting. "Is there something on your mind?"

"I don't know how I feel about you going back." Lay-Lay laid completely back so that her head was in his lap and she could see his face.

"You worried about me and Smoke?" Kyle's eyes wandered around the room while he remained silent. "I already know that's your problem. You don't even have to say it. Let me tell you something, you better get your mind right. You're my husband; I'm in this shit whole-heartedly. I wouldn't have married you if I still wanted that nigga." Lay-Lay sat up and turned his head so that he was facing her. "Tell me right now that you know I'm not going to cheat on you, emotionally or physically." He tried to snatch his head away but she held it tighter. "Tell me." If Kyle thought he was about to pull the insecure card on her, he was sadly mistaken.

"Kyle, if you don't open your mouth and talk right now, I will punch you in the face."

"I know you still have feelings for that nigga. I saw you texting him the other night at Jones' house."

"So. I texted his ass a picture of Lana to let him know he'd been cheating on me with a married woman. I don't want Smoke's cheating ass!"

"Lay-Lay, you're not about to sit here and tell me you don't still have feelings for this dude. The shit doesn't go away that fast."

"Well you married me knowing I still felt something for Smoke. Obviously you trust me enough to know I'm not about to jeopardize what we have over some damn feelings." Lay-Lay watched as his chest heaved up and down. *Oh he mad!* She wondered for a brief second had she gone too far, but then let it go. If they were going to have a healthy marriage, then he needed to be able to tolerate how slick her mouth could be. She was about to call his name again before he jumped off the couch and left. Not one to easily be intimidated, she followed right behind him. He was in their room looking through his drawers when she came in.

"Where do you think you're going?" He didn't say anything; he just kept grabbing clothes. "I said where are you going, Kyle Taylor?" She blocked his path once he grabbed his sneakers from under the bed.

"Move Shalaya. I'm going to the gym."

"No sir, I don't think you are." He looked like he wanted to push his way past her again, but changed his mind. Instead, he asked her to move again. "Nope. I'm not moving until you talk to me. If you want to throw a tantrum, that's fine with me, but you gon' throw it at home. You're not leaving this house. I can bet you that." Lay-Lay stood back on her leg and crossed her arms over her chest for emphasis. She stared him directly in his eyes until he turned his head. When he turned back around, he was smiling.

"Man move out my way, girl."

"Make me." Although she was just talking, Kyle picked her up by both of her arms and slammed her on the bed. Lay hopped back up no soon as he threw her down. "I bet you won't do it again." Kyle reached to grab her again and when he did, she grabbed him into a headlock. When he tossed her on the bed, she pulled him down with her. She proceeded to punch him in the side of the head playfully. This lasted until he started tickling her.

"Nooooo. Kyle, stop please," she laughed uncontrollably until he stopped. When he was done, it took her a second to catch her breath again. He sat on the bed looking at her until she sat up next to him.

"I don't know who your little ass thinks you are. Better yet, who do you think I am? I'm not Smoke. You're not about to talk to me like you run something around here. I'm the man up in this house, and you better learn to act like it."

"Yes sir daddy."

"Call me daddy again," Kyle said breathlessly. Lay-Lay got up and began to back up towards the door, biting her lip.

"I'm sorry for acting up, daddy. I think I might need a spanking." She winked when Kyle dropped the clothing he was holding onto the bed before standing to his feet. Lay-Lay carefully took in all of the sexiness wrapped in his tall, muscular body. His smile was bright as he inched closer to her.

"I think I'm about to start charging you for the dick. You ride this muthafucka like a mad woman. Every time I look around, your ass back up here again," Kyle said as he grabbed a handful of the hard length stretching down his thigh. *Lawd help me!* Lay thought as she turned serious. Kyle's body mixed in with the things he was saying, and the way he was saying it, had her on fire. She was done playing games. She ran to him and jumped up into his arms. He held her up by her butt as he led them to the bed, where they stayed for hours.

Chapter 5

"I know you wouldn't cheat on me, Shalaya."

Lay-Lay looked at him. "Say what now?" Kyle laughed, because he knew she'd heard him. She just wanted to play games.

"I know you wouldn't cheat. I've never thought that. I just don't want you to connect with him emotionally. That'll mess us up."

"You could have said this earlier, but I understand. I won't even put myself in that type of situation. Jaylen and I have nothing to talk about, I promise. We're friends, nothing more."

With a brief head nod, he turned the music back up. They were headed to the furniture store so she could finish decorating the house before he left for deployment. She was on her head to decorate, and he was going to let her. It wasn't like he didn't have the money. On top of that, she was his wife. That was her house too. After they left there, he was taking her on post to get her enrolled in DEERS He wanted to make sure she had all the military rights she was entitled to.

"My deployment is nine months. You sure you're going to be alright while I'm gone?"

"No, I'ma cry every day."

"You'll be fine. We've done this about three times already."

"It's not the same. I had Smoke to distract me then." She looked at him with a sly smirk before looking back out of the window. Kyle grabbed her hand and held it while they drove.

*****

Smoke had just left Kristen's house, and was pulling into his driveway when he noticed Lana's car parked in his driveway. He sighed heavily before getting out. He was not in the mood to deal with her drama today. He hadn't had sex in almost three weeks, and it was starting to get to him. Kristen was still on her little tirade, and Lay-Lay wasn't even a possibility. He'd cancelled all the rest of his hoes when he thought they were getting back together. After pulling the blunt from his ashtray, Smoke lit it and took a few pulls before getting out.

He was going to need to be a little intoxicated in order to deal with her. Before he could even finish smoking, she was getting out of her car. He sat there for a minute, not even bothering to roll the window down. She shifted from one leg to another before knocking on his glass. That pissed him off. He paid too much money for his things for a hoe that's in her feelings to mess it up. Smoke put out his blunt and opened the door. She backed away to give him room to step out.

"Why have you been ignoring my calls?"

"I figured you and your husband needed time to talk."

Lana rolled her eyes up towards the sky. "I knew that bitch was going to run her mouth. I bet she couldn't wait to tell you that."

Smoke laughed as he took in Lana's anger. "You serious right now?"

"Hell yeah I'm serious."

"Lana, you sound stupid as fuck. Of course she was going to tell me. We've been rocking forever. Whether we together or not, that's my nigga. We gon' always be friends. She don't owe your ass no type of loyalty. Shit, I been fucking your ass practically the whole time I've been with her. You thought she wouldn't take this opportunity to get your ass back?"

"I'm just saying though. That wasn't her place."

"Just like it wasn't your fucking place to call the police on her. It's not your place to be at my fucking house right now, but you're here."

Lana looked dumbfounded. She was about to say something else, but he walked past her and up to his porch. He could hear her following him, but he didn't know why. She was not coming in.

"I'm leaving my husband. I told him I wanted a divorce. I want to be with you." The look on Smoke's face had to have told her how stupid she was long before his mouth even opened.

"I don't know why you did that. We aren't about to be together. This shit is over. I got other stuff I'm trying to do right now."

Lana immediately began to cry and plead her case. This was exactly the type of drama he didn't have time for. In no way, shape, or form, was he trying to hear the nonsense coming out of her mouth, so instead of standing there watching her theatrics, he went in his house and slammed the door. He could hear her out there screaming like a lunatic for him to open the door, but that wasn't happening. His phone beeped with a text from Kristen as he headed for his bedroom.

She needed some more vitamins to help with her sickness. As much as he hated to do this, he grabbed a bottle of water and headed back out the door. Even with all the craziness sitting on his front porch, his kids came first. He had to get Kristen her pills, so he was about to have to deal with crazy ass Lana. What woman in her right mind would leave her husband for her side nigga? Smoke couldn't help but to laugh, because that was dumb as hell on her part.

"Lana, get your ass up and go call your husband. Tell that nigga you made a mistake or something."

"No, because I didn't. I only want you."

"Bitch you dun' lost your mind. Get your ass up and go home. I ain't got time for this shit."

"Smoke, don't do this!" she yelled as she ran behind him. He tried his best to dodge her, but she grabbed onto his jacket and wouldn't let go. He tried everything he could to get her off him, but she didn't budge until he slapped her. She must have had him confused with her husband, grabbing all over his shit like that.

"Take your ass home."

She grabbed the side of her face and hobbled to her car. He didn't feel the least bit of remorse. She should have left when he told her to. It had been thirty minutes since he'd gotten Kristen's message, and he was just pulling up to her house. When he walked in, she was lying on the sofa and she looked horrible. Her skin was a little ashy, and her hair was a mess.

"Damn girl, lil mama tearing your ass up."

Instead of saying anything, she shot him a bird instead. He grabbed her some water before coming back to make her take the pills.

"You want me to take Caleb, so you can get some rest?"

"Nah, y'all can stay."

"You sure?"

Kristen nodded her head weakly. "Yeah. Come lay down with me."

"Girl, you look like hell. What make you think I want to lay down with you looking like that?"

Kristen chuckled lightly as she drank more of her water. Smoke stood up and removed his boots and hoodie before squeezing on the sofa behind her. He wrapped her small body in his arms and pulled her close to him. She was sleep within seconds. Smoke watched her sleep while he rubbed on her round belly.

"You have to stop giving your mama such a hard time, lil girl. She ain't tough like daddy, you have to take it easy on her." Kristen's stomach began to jump and shift like crazy the more he talked. He could already see his baby was going to be a daddy's girl. He laid there watching TV and holding Kristen as she slept. Caleb eventually came downstairs, only to fall asleep on Kristen's legs.   A
few hours later Smoke woke up, not even realizing he'd fell asleep. He looked over, and Kristen and Caleb were both still sleeping. As he lay cuddled up on the couch with his little family, he realized maybe being with Kristen full time wouldn't be so bad. After all the shit he'd put her through, she'd stayed down with him. Maybe the family man life wouldn't be too bad.

*****

It was the Friday before Christmas, and Lay-Lay was lying in her apartment alone. She'd just gotten back to Atlanta a little over an hour ago, and she was immensely depressed. Kyle's unit had left for Syria two days ago, and she'd been a mess ever since. Every time she thought about having to spend nine months here without him, she got even sadder–if that was even possible. She had just gotten out of the shower, and was laid across her bed. She hadn't even attempted to put on any clothing, because she didn't plan on going anywhere.

She had no plans of moving any time soon, or at least that's what she thought. A few seconds after she began to cry again, her doorbell rang. Whoever it was had started to knock as well. Lay slow poked out of bed and wrapped her towel back around her. When she checked the peephole, she smiled for the first time in almost forty-eight hours. It was baby Dallas. Morgan was holding him up to the peephole.

"What y'all two hoes doing here?"

"We came to get your ass out this house. Kyle called me before he left and told me that he was worried about you. Now I see why," Morgan said, handing off baby Dallas to Lay-Lay. Jade followed behind her with Daylen.

"Bitch you need to get your life. Over here acting like that damn boy dun' died or something." Jade mushed her head as they all sat down on the sofa.

"I'm trying y'all. I just miss him already. I don't know what I'ma do the next couple of months."

"You're going to get your life together and stop moping around like a psycho. You and Kyle have been through this a million times before."

"It's different this time. We weren't really together back then."

Jade and Morgan tried continuously to get her to see the brighter side of the picture but she didn't, so they decided to leave it alone.

"Well at least get dressed and come over to the house. King is cooking, and we're hanging out and playing cards and stuff. I know you dun' got all cozy with Kyle's fine ass in South Carolina, but you can still kick it with your day ones."

Lay-Lay smiled at Jade before agreeing with her about how fine Kyle was.

"Whatever. I don't have the time to deal with y'all nasty asses. Lay, get dressed so we can go," Morgan said as she began to nurse Daylen. Lay got up and handed Jade baby Dallas.

"Here, get boobie boy so I can put on some clothes." She went into her room and threw on a pair of jeans and a black True Religion hoodie. She combed her wrap down before putting her boots and jacket on. Once she grabbed her phone and charger, they left. They were down the stairs and almost to Morgan's car when she stopped.

"Let me find out my brother in love. Jade, he left his truck with this bitch."

"That's how you do it, bestie." Jade high fived Lay as she walked to Kyle's truck. "Let's ride in Lay-Lay's car, Morgan."

"I got the car seats, though."

"Girl so! Come on. We'll strap them in the backseat of their Uncle and Auntie's truck."

"Man I swear, y'all so extra. Come on." Lay-Lay laughed and hit the unlock button so they could get in. She moved some of Kyle's things around so that they could all fit comfortably. Once the babies were locked in, Lay-Lay purposely pulled off fast, making Morgan fall to the front of the truck.

"Damn Lay, slow your butt down."

Jade and Lay-Lay burst out laughing, while Morgan tried to fix her hair in the mirror. When they pulled up to Jade and King's house, there were cars everywhere. Jade had to quickly explain that Zion, Bam's little sister, and KB were there too. Of course being that she was so nosey, Jade had to go into extra detail as to why Zion was now dating Bam's sister. When they finally got into the house, everybody greeted her with love. They were all so happy to see here doing better. She was greeted with hugs and conversation from everybody.

"What up lil sis, you feeling better?" King asked as he grabbed her into a side hug with Dallas, Zion, and KB following immediately behind him.

"Damn, y'all niggas must have really missed me? I ain't been gone but two weeks. Y'all gon' really miss me when I move up there permanently."

"Hold on, permanently? When you decided this?"

"A couple of days ago. I'm moving with Kyle when he comes back."

"No Lay-Lay, you can't do that," Jade whined. Lay walked over and rubbed her small baby bump.

"Everybody else live with their man, why I can't live with mine?"

"Don't listen to her Lay-Lay. Daddy baby just got her all emotional and shit," King walked past and kissed Jade's forehead as he headed into the living room. All the men had settled into the living room while Morgan, Jade, Lay-Lay, and Tasheena congregated in the room the Jade was decorating for her baby.

"So Miss Tasheena, you must think you family now? Last time I seen you, you were working with the enemy," Lay-Lay said.

Tasheena fidgeted with her hands. "I know. I'm sorry about that. I was just caught up."

Lay-Lay laughed at how nervous Tasheena got after she'd spoken to her.

"I'm just playing, girl. You good. Zion is my little brother, so if you with him than you're fam." Lay had just got done talking when she heard two familiar voices. She shushed her friends so she could hear better. Just like she'd thought, it was Smoke, and he had Kristen's ass with him. Jade looked just as shocked as Lay-Lay. She knew Smoke was coming, but she had no idea he was bringing Kristen with him. Lay mouthed the words *I'ma slap y'all* as she pointed her finger at Jade and Morgan. They both held their hands up in mock surrender.

"Let's go speak," Jade said, grabbing Lay-Lay's hand and pulling her up the hallway.

"Whose big ass truck is that outside?" she heard Smoke ask just as she and the rest of the girls rounded the corner.

"Mine."

The look on Smoke and Kristen's face was priceless. He looked shocked to see her, whereas Kristen just looked annoyed.

"Damn girl, what you doing here? I ain't know you were back in the city."

"I'm chilling. Hey Kristen," Lay-Lay said, disregarding Smoke's other comments. Kristen waved her hand, but didn't open her mouth. "You getting big, girl. Congratulations on y'all daughter. I'm actually glad I didn't kill her that day," Lay smirked

"Bitch you shot out for that shit," Kristen spat. Clearly, Lay had ruffled her feathers with that remark.

"Calm all that down over there, lil baby. It's not necessary." The whole living room was quiet as they waited for what might happen. Little did they know, Lay-Lay had moved on from that. She wasn't even thinking about Smoke and Kristen's ass. She had already known that's who he would run to once they broke up; he always did.

"Hey man!" Lay-Lay squealed when she noticed Caleb holding on to Smoke's leg. His smile mirrored hers as soon as he noticed she was talking to him. He let go of Smoke's leg and ran straight to her. She kissed all over his chubby cheeks as she held him. He was too busy playing in her hair to kiss her back.

"Is everybody ready to eat?" Jade asked. That was the cue they'd all been waiting on. People scattered around the house fixing plates and finding seats. Lay had just sat down when she heard her phone ring. She almost dropped her plate trying to get to it.

"Damn girl, slow down before you kill yourself," Smoke said.

"Shut up," she said as she answered her phone. There was a lot of static at first, then she heard Kyle's deep voice over the phone line.

"Hey gorgeous. You miss me?"

"Yes baby! You have no idea. You okay?"

"Yeah, we just landed. I wanted to call and let you know I'm here and I'll call you as soon as I can. Relay my message to my mom and Morgan. I love you bae, call you soon."

"I love you too. Be safe."

"Give me a kiss, Shalaya."

Her eyes misted with water as she kissed loudly into the phone. When she hung up, Smoke's eyes were burning a hole into her head, but she didn't care. She hopped off the floor and ran to the bathroom. She splashed water on her face a few times before drying it again. When her hands were dry, she dug into her sweatshirt, digging for the necklace she had on. On Tuesday, after getting all of her military spousal stuff done, she and Kyle spent the rest of the day at the mall. While they were there, they got his wedding band made into a necklace. The jeweler put it on a necklace made out of white gold with a heart pendant inside of it. Kyle didn't want to lose it, but insisted on her keeping it. This was the best idea they'd came up with.

She'd been staring at it since he left. Since they'd decided to keep their marriage a secret for now, she had no plans of wearing hers. With her fingers clasped tightly around his ring, she leaned against the wall. The thought of him never coming back was driving her insane. She'd been researching everything happening in Syria and Iraq since he'd told her that's where he would be going. The thing that bothered her the most was the fact that he had to be directly in the line of fire. Not only was he a surgeon in a war zone, but a trauma surgeon at that. He would be the first person they called if something went wrong. This Army wife life was hard as hell already.

"I knew she was in here crying," Jade said as she, Morgan, and Tasheena walked into the bathroom.

"Close the door, Sheena," Morgan said as she took a seat on the counter. Tasheena sat down on the side of the bathtub and made herself comfortable.

"Shalaya, are you pregnant too?" Jade asked.

"No Jade, I'm not. I'm just sad. I don't want him to die."

"He's not going to die, Lay-Lay. Kyle is one of the best soldiers in the world. My brother will be fine. I used to be the same way when he first started leaving. I didn't start to feel better until I realized he came back every time. We'll get through this deployment together, sis."

"I know. It's just so hard this time. I miss him like crazy, and he hasn't even been gone a whole week yet."

"Nah bitch, you miss that dick like crazy. I got a good look at it that day they were at the basketball court. Jersey shorts don't lie, my nigga." Jade knew that would make her laugh. The girls had just stopped laughing when they heard a knock at the door.

"Y'all straight?"

"Yes Smoke, Shalaya is fine. She's just sad about her boyfriend being gone." All four of the ladies traded grins as they waited for his response. Lay gave Morgan a *thumbs up* for saying that. Before long, they heard him walk away. They all burst out laughing as soon as they heard him talking to King again.

"Morgan, you ain't got no sense. You probably hurt his feelings," Tasheena said.

"So; he hurt my sister feelings all the time." They all laughed and talked a little while longer before exiting the restroom. Once they got back inside, King had Daylen, Dallas had baby Dallas, and Smoke was holding Caleb.

"Aww, look at daddy daycare," Jade smiled as she took the baby from King. The moment she did, Daylen started to cry. King told Jade it was because she loved her uncle. Once everybody was seated and comfortable, Dallas turned on a movie. Lay-Lay looked around at everybody cuddled with their significant other and almost got sad again. The only other single person was KB, and he was texting. He was probably headed to see a female as soon as he left. Shortly into the movie, Lay-Lay was getting up to get her some more food when she heard Kristen ask Smoke to bring her some water.

"I'll get it if you want me to. I'm about to get me some more food," Lay said, reaching to grab the cup Kristen was holding. She pulled it back and shook her head.

"No thank you."

"Suit yourself then. I was just trying to be nice, but if you want your man in this kitchen with me by himself, then cool." Lay walked into the kitchen. *Dumb hoe!* She washed her hands and prepared to fix her some food when Smoke walked in behind her. Lay-Lay tried her best to pretend like she didn't see him, but he was being so extra. Every time she turned around, he was standing right up on her.

"What Jaylen?"

"You look nice."

"I look the same as I always look."

"Dang, that nigga got you not even wanting to speak to ya boy no more. I see he's buying you trucks and shit."

"Stop being bitter, Jaylen. That's his truck and I spoke to you when you and your family first came in."

He was smiling when she looked at him. He was caught and didn't have a word to say.

"You're a nigga through and through. You have no shame what so ever. Go back in that living room with your baby mama and leave me alone."

Smoke was half way out of the kitchen door when she saw him stop and turn around.

"You love him, Lay-Lay?"

"More than anything."

Smoke's facial expression was one she was all too familiar with. This was mainly because she'd seen it on her own too many times to count. You could recognize hurt on anyone, and right now Smoke was wearing it pitifully. After a few hours, it had started getting late and everybody was preparing to leave. Jade begged Lay-Lay to spend the night, but she continuously told her no. She wanted to be in her own house for a change. She hadn't been there for a few weeks. She watched Smoke open the door and help Kristen inside the car before snapping Caleb in. She would be lying if she said it didn't bother her, but she would be fine. Now that their time was over, maybe he and Kristen's could finally begin.

*****

Trina's "Fuck Love" was blasting through the speakers in Lay-Lay's living room as she did her homework. It had been two months already, and she was doing a lot better. She'd started her first semester of classes at Emory Law, and she'd been talking to Kyle regularly. Things were actually getting better in her life–minus the fact that Valentine's Day was in two days, and she had no one to spend it with. She'd recently joined a few deployed spouses groups on Facebook and had learned a lot. It was helpful to talk to women that were in her same position. One of the groups was made up of the women from Kyle's unit, while the others were just Army wives in general.

Colonel Greene's wife called and checked on her at least twice a week. She also made sure to update her when she hadn't heard form Kyle. In one of the groups, one of the wives made a post about sending a care package to her husband for the holidays. That piqued Lay's interest, because she hadn't known that was possible. Once she finished her homework, she, Jade, Morgan, and Tasheena were going shopping for the box she was making. Her brain was overflowing with ideas for his package. He probably wouldn't get it until after the holiday, but it was better late than never.

After three more long hours of reading and writing information from her law book, she was able to close it and get her day started. She got dressed, did her hair, and called her friends to see where they were. Jade told her they were down the street, so while she waited she walked to check her mail. Upon sitting her mail down, her doorbell rang. Assuming it was her girls, she opened the door without checking her peephole.

"Hello ma'am, I have a delivery for you." Lay-Lay looked at the short man dressed in a white and red uniform holding his clipboard.

"From who?"

"Please sign here." After telling her he would be right back, he handed her the clipboard and walked away. Lay-Lay stood there looking over her balcony, trying to see where he was going. The only thing she saw was the large white florist truck. She sat the clipboard on the banister and walked back inside. Just as she comfortable on the sofa, he appeared again along with two other men. They were all carrying large bouquets of roses.

"Where should we put these?"

"Just put them anywhere they'll fit," Morgan said as she, Jade, and Tasheena came through the door.

"Thank you so much. You can sit them on the table."

"We're not finished yet ma'am." Lay-Lay couldn't stop smiling as she watched the men make four more trips to the truck. By the time they, left her home was filled with red roses.

"Open the card so we can see who they're from." Lay grabbed the card Jade was handing her.

"They better be from my brother."

"And if they're not?"

"I'ma slap your cheating ass." Lay-Lay rolled her eyes at Morgan and opened the card.

To my beautiful and gorgeous girl, I just want you to know you're in my heart, you're in my soul, and you're on my mind. I'll be missing you terribly until we're together again. –Kyle

"AWWWW SHALAYAAA!" Jade was smiling as she grabbed Tasheena's arm. "That was so sweet."

"It sure was. I wish Zion would send me flowers with a sweet card like that."

"Girl, you got my brother sprung," Morgan walked across the room to where Lay-Lay was standing.

"Kyle knows how sensitive I am. I don't know why he sent me these," she wiped her eyes as her doorbell rang again. Morgan answered it since she was the closest. There was a man standing there dressed in an all-black tuxedo. He stepped inside the door and said special delivery. All eyes were on him as he begun to sing "Teach Me How to Love" by Musiq Soulchild. Lay-

Lay slid down to the floor as he sang. All she could think about was how much thought Kyle had put into his gift. This was the perfect song for her and Kyle. They'd been through so much while being apart that they both needed to learn to love the right way.

"Shalaya, I'm a friend of Kyle's and he wants you to have this." The guy singing pulled a mint green Tiffany's bag from behind his back and tried to pass it to her, but Morgan grabbed it first. The singer smiled before telling the ladies Happy early Valentine's Day and exiting. Tasheena and Jade rushed Morgan to open the card. Lay-Lay was still sitting on the floor marveling at the roses. She had never had anyone do something this sweet for her. She got up to sit on the sofa, as did the other girls while Morgan pulled the card and gift out of the bag. They were all so anxious; Jade opened the gift while Morgan read the card.

Shalaya I know how much you love now and laters, so I'll give you this now with the promise that later will be exceedingly better. I love you sweet girl –Your Husband

Jade slapped her forehead and lay back on the couch. "Lawd! I should have gotten Kyle first!"

"Husband huh?" Morgan smiled at Lay-Lay. She smiled and took the gift box from Jade. It was the most beautiful charm bracelet. It held three charms. One was the letter K with little diamonds on the inside of it, the second was a wedding ring, and the third was a heart shaped lock. This promptly became her new favorite piece of jewelry.

"Chile, get your butt up and get dressed so we can go." Jade walked into the kitchen to check her fridge for food.

"I'm telling you, sitting over there looking at that bracelet like it's gon' disappear."

Lay shot Jade and Morgan both birds as she headed to change. She had just removed her shirt when she heard Morgan yell her name. She ran into the living room to make sure nothing was wrong. Morgan had screamed like there was a fire or something. In her bra and gym shorts, she checked to see what Morgan wanted.

She stopped in front of them. "What's up?"

One of Morgan's eyebrows was raised in confusion as she held up a little black card. Shalaya was still confused as to why Morgan had yelled. What was the problem?

"What's that?"

"It's a new American Express black card for a Shalaya Taylor. You know her?"

Lay-Lay's stomach dropped when she read her new last name written across the bottom of the card. She was about to have to tell them about the marriage now. Hopefully they wouldn't be too mad at her for keeping it a secret. She stood silent for a minute, looking from Jade to Morgan. It didn't matter if Tasheena knew or not. They were both staring her down waiting for an answer. Instead of talking, Lay-Lay went to her room, grabbed her necklace with Kyle's band on it, and her ring from the jewelry box on the dresser. When she returned, she placed a piece of jewelry in each of their hands.

"I know y'all ain't married?" Morgan asked in disbelief.

"Yeah. We got married about a week or two before he left." Lay-Lay looked at Morgan, waiting for her to say something else.

"Congratulations bestie. Why didn't you tell us?" Jade wrapped her arm around Lay-Lay's neck and hugged her. Morgan stood in the same spot with Lay-Lay's ring in her hand.

"We just wanted to keep it a secret for a while. Honestly, we needed some time to get used to it ourselves. Kyle thought it would be best if we waited."

"I don't know whether to be happy or slap the piss out of you for not telling me. Now we're real sisters," Morgan beamed. Lay breathed a little sigh of relief. She wasn't sure what Morgan was going to think about everything. Tasheena hugged her once Jade and Morgan finally let her go.

"No fair, now you and Morgan are real sisters and I'm just y'all friend. I want to be y'all sister too," Jade poked her bottom lip and began to pout.

"Jade, shut up. We've been sisters long before my brother ever chose to marry this lil ghetto hoe."

"Bitch, that's Mrs. Ghetto Hoe to you. I's married now boo." Lay-Lay slid her ring on her finger and flaunted around for her friends to see. She'd missed wearing it. Once the initial shock wore off, they all huddled around comparing the sizes of their rings.

"I'm jealous, man. All y'all married, and all I am is Zion's girlfriend."

"You have to crawl before your walk, baby girl" Jade pinched Tasheena's arm. Morgan nudged Jade's shoulder.

"Girl, what you say? All we've been through with these niggas, they just better had married us. Give it some time; Zion will be ready. Y'all are just so young. Don't rush it."

"Well some of us have been through it all with our husbands. This heffa just ran straight into paradise with Kyle's ass. He's been good from day one. He's spoiling the mess out of her. You see all this mess? Roses, Tiffany's, a fucking black card! This hoe just spoiled," Jade laughed as she and Tasheena looked around at all of the stuff Kyle had sent.

"I been told Lay-Lay to fuck with a real nigga, but she wouldn't listen to me. Kyle has been sweet our whole life. I knew he would be a good man to whoever was smart enough to keep him. If you ask me, I think we've all done pretty good for ourselves. We've graduated, got married, and remained friends. We're on that good shit."

Jade and Lay-Lay couldn't have agreed with Morgan more. She was absolutely right. They eventually got themselves together and headed out. They spent the entire afternoon shopping, and had even stopped to eat. Lay-Lay hadn't really wanted to give Tasheena a chance, but surprisingly she actually liked her. She reminded her of a miniature Jade. Lay was happy that Jade had taken her under her wing. She could groom Tasheena into a real woman. She was already experienced from her previous relationship, but she'd become more knowledgeable hanging with them. There was more to life than just being the girlfriend of a street nigga. They were headed to the car when Morgan begged to go in Children's Place. They were having a sale, and she wanted to get the twins some more clothes.

"Lay-Lay, go see if they have something that look like this in Daylen's size," Morgan held up the dark blue baby boy overalls. She always made sure the twins clothing were similar. When she was able to find gender-neutral clothing, she was on cloud nine. Lay-Lay grabbed Jade and walked to the girl's side. She was scanning through the racks searching for Daylen's clothing when an all too familiar smell invaded her nostrils.

If she'd known what she was about to see she would have kept her head down. Smoke and Kristen were at the counter with a pile of clothes for their daughter. They actually looked happy. She was holding her stomach while his arm rested around her shoulders. Lay watched them interact lovingly. The whole scene would have been cute had it not been her ex-boyfriend, with the baby mama he'd been cheating on her with since they'd been together.

"Come on *Mrs.* Taylor," Jade put emphasis on the word Mrs. when she grabbed Lay-Lay's arm.

"Nah. Let's go speak." Lay-Lay picked up the closest newborn outfit she could find and went to the counter, dragging Jade with her.

"Well, aren't y'all the cutest little thing," Lay-Lay's voice was filled with sarcasm.

Smoke and Kristen both turned around to see her. Smoke smiled and Kristen frowned. Lay-Lay smiled, because she'd expected both of their reactions.

"What you doing in here?" Smoke asked as he handed the cashier his card.

"Buying my step-daughter some clothes." Jade snickered when Lay held up the little newborn outfit. Kristen rolled her eyes and crossed her arms over her large stomach.

"She doesn't need it. Her daddy already bought enough stuff."

"Kristen, listen girl, take this little outfit. I'm trying to be nice. I'm over this foolishness. It's apparent y'all are about to be together, and I want us all to be on good terms. Just like I know, you know that he and I will forever be friends. I'm tired of beating your ass, let's just be friends." Lay-Lay stepped forward and smiled. Kristen looked at her sideways before looking at Smoke and Jade, then back at Lay-Lay. They all looked at her waiting for an answer.

"You're probably faking it, but whatever. We're good."

"Kristen, I'm really not. I'm not with Smoke anymore, so there's no reason for me not to like you."

"That doesn't mean you don't still love him."

"I love him, but so? I love my husband more." Jade gasped as Smoke and Kristen finally took notice to the large rock that adorned her left finger. Lay thought she saw steam coming from Smoke's ears he was so mad. He snatched her hand so he could get a good look at her hand.

"Yo, you married this dude?"

"Yes Jaylen, I did."

"For what? Y'all ain't even been together that long." Smoke was starting to get loud, so Lay-Lay backed up some. Kristen, on the other hand, grabbed onto his arm.

"Smoke, calm down in this store. You're too loud." Smoke didn't acknowledge what she'd said; instead, he snatched his arm away and stared at Lay-Lay. If she hadn't known he was more hurt than angry, she might have been scared. He was looking at her like he wanted to kill her.

"I'm sorry." Lay-Lay genuinely was sorry. She never wanted to hurt Smoke, but she had to think about herself first. She couldn't live the rest of her life worrying about his feelings. Had he worried about hers half as much as she worried about his, they would probably still be together. They were no longer together; she was in love with Kyle. Once the words left her mouth, his mood softened. He looked at her for a long time, before grabbing the bags and walking away. The tears in his eyes almost made her feel bad about telling him.

Kristen grabbed the remaining bag. "Congratulations Lay-Lay. You probably shouldn't have told him like that, but he'll be fine."

"Yeah he will. His pride is just hurt. Give him some of that pregnant butt and he'll be back to normal in no time."

Kristen laughed and took the bag of clothes Lay-Lay had just bought and left the store. Jade walked to Lay-Lay.

"You were wrong for that. I think he was about to cry."

"I don't care, Jade. I have cried plenty of days. Smoke is a grown man; he better move on. How you think it would have made me feel to see him in here playing house with Kristen had I not had Kyle?"

"You right."

"I know. Let's go"

Chapter 6

"Stop playing and show me."

"Nah girl. It's people in here."

"I don't care about those people. Make them get out," Lay-Lay smiled at the screen. She and Kyle were on their nightly Skype date, and she wanted to be nasty. She'd been trying to convince Kyle to show her his dick since the call had begun, but he wouldn't. It had been almost four months since he'd been gone, and she was sexually frustrated. She'd stopped at Jade and King's house earlier and heard them having sex, and immediately got mad. Lay laughed as she thought about it. Those two clowns didn't even have the decency to be quiet while she was there. Lay watched Kyle say something to the other two men in his room before turning back around.

"You told them to leave?"

"Yeah. You made me."

"I knew you loved me. Show me the goodies." Lay-Lay's smile was big and bright.

"You go first." Lay-Lay willingly pulled up his shirt she was wearing, putting her large breasts on the camera. Unlike him, she didn't have a problem being freaky. Aside from him being her man, it wasn't like he hadn't seen it all before. When she saw him smiling, she did a quick spin to show him her butt in the cute thong panties she was wearing. "See I knew this was a bad idea."

"Why you say that?"

"Because now my dick hard and there's nothing you can do about it."

"I know right! Show it to me anyway." Lay-Lay had just pulled her shirt back down when her room door opened. In walked Jade and Morgan. "Shit! Y'all scared me to death." She had forgotten she'd given them a key. After leaving Jade's house, she'd called and said her and Morgan would be over later. Being on the phone with Kyle had caused it to completely slip her mind.

"Who is that?"

"Your sister and Jade's pregnant ass."

"That's Kyle?" Morgan ran to the computer so she could see him on the screen. They smiled at each other as Lay-Lay pushed her out of the way.

"Y'all are going to have to catch up on your own time. My husband and I were in the middle of Skype sex." Jade plopped down on the bed while Morgan scrunched her nose up, telling them how nasty they were. Jade, on the other hand, didn't care. She'd told them to go ahead, she didn't mind watching.

"Man, y'all are a trip. I'll talk to you later, baby. These guys are about to come back anyway."

"No. It's still your turn. Please, can I have just one peek?"

"Make your friends leave first." Morgan shot Kyle a bird as she got off the bed.

"Y'all nasty, we'll be in the living room."

Once the door was closed, Lay-Lay's smiling face was all in the screen. She could see Kyle laughing at her as he unbuckled the camo uniform pants he was wearing. He looked behind him a few times before he pulled his stiff manhood out and held it in his hand. Lay-Lay's jaw almost dropped. It had been so long that she almost forgot how big it was.

"Damn Kyle, maybe this was a bad idea," Lay-Lay stuck her lip out and pretended to pout.

"Show me something, Shalaya." Lay-Lay already knew what he meant, so she leaned backwards in the chair and propped her leg up on the side of the desk so he could see her wet center. It was freshly waxed, and was sitting nicely in her Vicky Secrets. She heard Kyle suck wind in through his teeth before mumbling a few curse words. She moved the seat of her panties to the side so he could get a good view before running her fingers through her wetness.

It thrilled her to see him

stroking himself while watching her. She could feel her orgasm building, so she sped up. The faster she went, the faster he went. Before long her legs were shaking as her orgasm took over her body. She bit down on her bottom lip to muffle her moans. If she knew Jade and Morgan, they were probably outside of the door listening. As she tried to catch her breath, she noticed Kyle was doing the same thing. He'd just thrown a towel onto the floor before looking up and smiling at her.

"That's the type of stuff that makes daddy miss home," Kyle buckled his pants back up before blowing her kisses through the camera.

"I know. I miss you so much. I can't wait until you come back. Six months down, three more to go baby."

"I'll be there soon. I love you."

"I love you too."

That big beautiful smile she loved so much flashed across the screen before it went blank. She shut off her computer and fixed the shirt she was wearing. When she went into the living room, Jade and Morgan both gave her a funny look.

"I don't know why y'all looking crazy. Y'all already know how I gets down, and Morgan I'm sorry to tell you, but your brother's a freak." Jade walked into the kitchen behind Lay-Lay.

"I hope you wash your nasty hands."

"Oh bitch, don't do that. I heard you and King's ass earlier. Don't let Morgan make you forget. Y'all hoes kill me, acting like y'all good. I have been there with both of y'all hoes at some point while y'all were tricking off, so calm all that down."

Jade rubbed her large belly and waddled back into the living room. "I was trying to get King to break my water or something. I'm tired of being pregnant. This little boy needs to come on." Jade was now nine months and getting more impatient than any other pregnant woman Lay-Lay had ever met. She was so hormonal and moody; she was getting hard to deal with.

They teased her all the time about having him. Although she was pretty pregnant, just like Morgan had been, her attitude was way worse. The girls sat around and talked for a few hours until Morgan had to leave to get the twins from Dallas. His father was in town, and they'd taken the babies to the park. Lay-Lay walked Jade to the door and watched her get into her car before closing and locking her door.

*****

It was five in the morning, and very dark outside. The wind blew sand all around as they walked. The 113-degree weather was only adding to the stress of this mission. Kyle and his unit were heading deeper into the city, and it was stressful. They still had a lot of ground in Syria left to cover, but it had to be done. The Islamic extremists had begun to take over more land, despite the various airstrike attempts by the United States. Kyle had known all along it would come to a point like this, but he had to keep pushing. They were there to do a job, and it had to be done. Mack was stationed on top of one of the buildings across from the one they were about to enter. He was one of the best snipers, so this eased Kyle's mind a little. They were being led by the 227th Infantry unit from Schofield Barracks, Hawaii. They'd gone on several missions since being here, but this was supposed to be the most important.

They'd gotten word that this house was filled with an array of Islamic leaders that were deeply involved in the ISIS matter. Kyle looked up when the leader held his hand up counting. No words were spoken as he held up three fingers. The door was kicked open, and they all filed inside. The entire unit had gotten in and began to spread around the dark house. Kyle walked into the kitchen with his weapon drawn when he saw the flashing red light. He yelled for his unit to run, but it was too late.

BOOM!

The raggedy building burst into flames.

*****

It was the last day of classes for this week, and Lay-Lay had just turned in her final assignment. Law

School was proving to be a little harder than she'd expected, but she was maintaining. It was challenging, but nothing she couldn't handle. Although she had the tendency to be a little ghetto and rowdy, she was a very smart girl. She'd made good grades this first semester, and planned to continue. She had just walked outside into the sunlight when her phone rang. It was from a number she didn't recognize. Normally she didn't answer for unfamiliar callers, but ever so often Kyle would call from different numbers, so she did.

"Hello?"

"Good afternoon ma'am. May I speak with Mrs. Taylor?"

Lay-Lay pressed her phone closer to one ear while plugging the other with her finger. "This is she. May I ask who is calling?"

"This is Captain Long. I'm with the 61st Infantry Regiment from Fort Jackson, South Carolina." There was a long stretch of silence; he was obviously waiting for her to say something.

Lay-Lay's heart began to beat faster while she tried catching the breath that had just left her body.

"I'm calling on behalf of Major Taylor's unit. He and his team entered an unsecure entity last night, and he was injured. It's not fatal, but he's in critical condition and he's being transported to the Landstuhl Regional Medical Center in Rheinland-Pfalz Germany."

Lay-Lay fell to her knees in the middle of the courtyard. People were walking past looking at her, but at the moment, nothing else mattered. Tears gathered in her eyes as she sat on the ground, a second from losing her mind. This is what she'd been dreading.

"When can I see him?"

"We're going to try to get him stable before sending him to a closer hospital. It should take no longer than forty-eight hours, depending on the extent of his injuries. I'm sorry, ma'am."

Lay-Lay knew he was still talking, but she hadn't heard anything else. After hearing that something had happened to Kyle, she was a mess. She could barely move. Her body felt like it weighed a ton. Her backpack and phone was cradled in her lap, and her hair had fallen slightly into her face. She didn't know how long she had been sitting in the middle of the courtyard before her phone started ringing again. She could tell it was Morgan by the ringtone. All she heard was screaming when she answered.

"Lay-Lay where are you?" King's deep voice bellowed through her cellphone speaker.

"At school." Lay-Lay was barely able to talk; her mouth was so dry from crying.

"Stay there. I'm coming to get you," King said as he hung up the phone. She'd undoubtedly popped into his mind after seeing the shape Jade and Morgan were in. Lay-Lay sat in the same spot, until she saw King and Dallas walking towards her.

"Come on Lay-Lay, get up. You have to get yourself together. They're going to need you to handle his business. Let's go," Dallas said as he picked her up from the ground.

She leaned on Dallas until they got to his truck. Once they'd helped her in and fastened her seatbelt, she looked out of the window until they pulled up to Jade and King's house. Inside, Jade and Morgan looked just as bad as she assumed she did. Morgan was sprawled out on the couch with a dazed out look on her face. Jade was rocking back and forth, holding her stomach. Lay-Lay grabbed her chest and sat on the sofa next to Morgan. Seeing them had put her right back into her feelings. She released a loud sigh and sat forward on her knees.

The living room was a mix between sad an awkward. Everyone was lost, with no idea what to do next. Lay sat back against the sofa again and rubbed her hands over her face. She was so worried she didn't know what else to do with herself. She stayed like this for another few minutes, just looking around at everybody. Seeing them all in such disarray made something in Lay-Lay click. She thought back on the day she almost took her own life, and how strong Kyle had been for her. The roles had flipped; it was her turn to be the strong one. In that moment, she snapped out of the slumber she was in and walked over to Morgan.

"Have they contacted your parents?" Morgan nodded. "Okay, I'm about to call this number back and see what's next. Go take a shower and get yourself together or something."

Lay-Lay pulled out her cell phone and dialed the number back. No one answered. She began to pace the floor, thinking of what might be next. Her father in law popped in her head, so she dialed his number.

"Hey Mr. Arty. Have you heard anything else?"

"Yes. He's in Germany right now. They're in the process of getting him transported here. He should be at his hospital in South Carolina within the next twenty-four hours. Hannah and I are booking our flights now."

Lay-Lay looked at her wrist and checked the time on her watch. "I'll meet you there."

"Okay sweetheart, we love you. Drive safe."

"Love you too." Lay-Lay hung up her phone and told King she needed to go to her house. He looked skeptical.

"What about your car?"

"Can one of y'all go get it? They're flying him back to Columbia. I need to go home, shower, change, and pack some things so I can be there when he gets there." Lay-Lay looked from King to Dallas to check for approval. They were each holding one of the twins, but giving her their undivided attention.

"All right, let us get Jade, Morgan, and the babies together, and we'll meet you at your house with your car. Here, drive my truck to your spot. I'll get it later," King handed her the keys.

She kissed baby Dallas and Daylen before darting out of the house. She sped the entire way home. She'd just walked into the door when her phone rang again. It was another unknown number.

She took a deep breath before answering. "Hello."

"Mrs. Taylor, this is Captain Long again. Major Taylor is being transported to Moncrief Hospital in South Carolina."

Lay-Lay took her keys out and opened the front door to her apartment. "I'll be there. Do you know how long it's going to take?"

"Not exactly. I'll call you when they land."

"Thank you, sir." She walked straight to her bedroom and grabbed her luggage from beneath her bed, while cradling the phone between her ear and shoulder.

"No problem, ma'am."

Lay-Lay threw the phone onto her bed and began packing her bags. She packed pretty much everything in her closet. She didn't plan on coming back any time soon. She'd email her professors, explaining the situation; hopefully they'd be generous enough to email her the assignments. She wasn't leaving South Carolina for anything until she knew that Kyle was okay. She dragged her bags to the front door and left them there until she was finished gathering everything she needed. She stood at the door, looking over her bags and trying to make sure she had everything.

"Oh shit! My flat irons!" Lay-Lay took off running to the back of the apartment in search of her favorite pair. She had at least six flat irons but there was only one pair that straightened her hair the way she liked it. She was headed back up her hallway when she heard knocks at her door. She opened it, and King and Dallas came in.

King picked up two of her bags. "Is this everything?"

"Yeah, it shouldn't be anything else. Just put it on the back of Kyle's truck."

"Where else you thought we was putting it?" Dallas grabbed two more bags. "This shit sure as hell couldn't fit in that little ass mustang."

Lay-Lay punched Dallas in the arm as she laughed for the first time all day. While the two of them moved her things out of the door, Lay-Lay moved around the house and made sure all of her lights and appliances were off. Once she was satisfied with the way things looked, she grabbed her bag of trash from the kitchen, her keys, and left. Her door was locked and her bags were packed. Lay-Lay got into Kyle's truck and prepared to pull off.

"We'll be right behind you. Your friends getting our stuff together, we're pulling out right after we pick them up and get some food." King pulled Lay-Lay into a hug and walked her to Kyle's truck.

"Be safe Lay-Lay Ali, we love your lil silly ass." Dallas gave her a hug after King let her go and closed the door to the truck.

"Awww, I love you y'all too. Hurry up and get on the road. I don't know if I can handle this by myself."

King took his keys from his pocket. "You're the same one that shot a nigga in the stomach for cheating on you; you can handle this little shit. Kyle straight. That man big as fuck, ain't shit banged him up that bad."

Lay-Lay laughed at King's comment and cranked up her truck. She was grateful for their attempts to make her feel better.

"My girls lucked up with y'all punk asses. I guess y'all all right."

Dallas and King made more jokes as they headed off to their cars. She looked in her rearview waiting for them to pull off, but they never did. Instead, they both beeped their horns for her to pull out before them. She plugged her iPod up and pulled out of her apartment complex. Once she was on the interstate, she pushed the gas until she was nearing one hundred miles per hour. She prayed for Kyle the entire ride there.

*****

"I need every nurse and free resident upstairs now. Someone call Ortho, and have them send Dr. Atkins. Scrub in and be ready to assist wherever you're needed." The Doctor ran past as he tied his scrub cap on.

Lay-Lay had just gotten off the elevator when a man in dark blue scrubs ran past, with a group of other doctors in lighter scrubs running behind him. He was barking out orders, and they looked to be the ones forced to follow them. That was definitely not what her nerves needed at the moment. She had tried calling Captain Long back but he hadn't answered, so she hadn't been updated on Kyle or his arrival yet. She figured she'd just ask once she got into the building. Lay-Lay leaned over the desk and waited for the woman to acknowledge her presence. When she continued to ignore her, Lay-Lay went ahead and asked her question.

"Has Major Taylor gotten here yet?"

The lady answered the phone like she hadn't heard a word Lay-Lay said. Lay-Lay took a breath and looked around for a second, trying to gather her thoughts. She needed to calm herself down before she got rowdy with the lady.

"Excuse me ma'am...ma'am excuse me." When she held up her finger, motioning for Lay-Lay to wait a minute, Lay-Lay lost every ounce of patience she had. "Look you old bitch, today is not the muthafuckin day. I tried asking you nicely to tell me has Major Taylor gotten here, and instead of telling me your ass is acting like you're fucking deaf." The lady opened her mouth like she was about to say something, but Lay-Lay snatched the phone from her hand before continuing. "Nah bitch, shut up. When I needed your ass to talk, you wasn't trying to say shit. You old but bitch you ain't dead yet, do your fucking job! Now I'ma ask you one more time, HAS...MAJOR...TAYLOR...GOTTEN...HERE YET!" Lay-Lay's voice carried through the small waiting room.

There were people were walking past looking at her, while others whispered amongst themselves. Lay could tell by the look on the woman's face she had gone a little hard on her, but today was not the day to test her patience. She felt bad when she noticed the water in the woman's eyes. Normally she wouldn't have done anything like that, because her mother had taught her to respect her elders, but her nerves were shot to hell and the woman's rudeness had pushed her over the edge. She watched the woman check the monitor before looking back up at her.

"He's upstairs being prepped for surgery. If you would like to catch him, you should go to the tenth floor right now. I'm not sure if you'll be allowed to see him, though."

"Thank you," Lay-Lay turned to walk away, but changed her mind and turned back around. "I'm sorry I spoke to you that way. I'm just really worried about Kyle."

The lady nodded her head, but didn't say anything. It was clear she was still a little sour, but she couldn't worry about that right now. She ran to the elevators she'd just gotten off and got back on, headed to the tenth floor. She looked around in search of somebody that could possibly provide her with answers. There were so many people running around that she didn't know who to stop first. She ran further down the hall and stopped at the small desk in the center of the floor.

"Excuse me, has Major Taylor's surgery started yet?"

The young girl looked from her computer to Lay-Lay. "Who are in relation to him, might I ask?"

Lawd please not another groupie. "Shalaya Taylor, his wife. Now, has his surgery started yet?"

"Ok, I just needed to be sure. Yes ma'am, he's in surgery as we speak. You can have a seat in the corner over there," the girl pointed towards a small sofa behind the nurse desk. "Or you can go to his office. The doctors will be out to update you shortly."

Lay-Lay nodded her head and walked over to the small sofa and sat down. She couldn't fathom sitting in Kyle's office right now. That small space filled with his scent would kill her. After talking to both Jade and Hannah and checking to see where they were, she got as comfortable as she could and waited. Every time a doctor came out, she would get nervous until she realized they weren't coming for her. This happened a few times before a tall, slender black man with a scrub cap on stopped in front of her. She didn't say anything or make eye contact with him, too afraid of what he might say.

"Mrs. Taylor, I'm Colonel Thomas. I'm the chief of surgery here, and I've been working along with your husband for a few years now. I've fixed him up for you; he's in HDU recovery right now." Lay-Lay finally looked up into his handsome face. He smiled and placed his hand on her shoulder. "I could walk you back to see him if you would like. However, there is something you should know."

Lay-Lay's heart felt like it had stopped in her chest as she waited for him to finish. "What?"

"His right leg was blown off during the explosion. I'm sorry."

Lay-Lay let out a small yell as she covered her mouth. Water clouded her vision as she tried to focus on this doctor's face. Painful moans escaped her lips as she rocked back and forth, crying silently. Wrapping her mind around the fact that he no longer had his leg was next to impossible, but she had to get herself together.

"I need to see him."

"Follow me. He hasn't awakened up from surgery yet, so he hasn't been informed about his leg. I can tell him, or I can stay with you while you do it."

Lay-Lay wiped the tears that continuously rolled down her cheeks. "I don't know if I can."

"If you can't, then I will. It's just easier hearing things like this from loved ones." He looked down at Lay-Lay's face and placed his hand gently on her shoulder.

Lay-Lay sniffed again. "Okay. Okay...I will do it."

Lay-Lay rested her fingertips on the side of her head, trying to ease the piercing ache that had recently started. She held on tightly to her cell phone and keys as they entered the HDU wing. It was the High Dependency Unit. They needed to monitor Kyle a little closer due to his injuries. Her heart began to speed up the closer they got to the glass doors that separated the rooms from each other. Colonel Thomas stopped in front of one of the doors and turned to look at her.

"You ready?"

"Not really, but let's go."

Colonel Thomas slid the glass door back and walked in, with her directly behind him. Lay-Lay didn't think she could look at him right away, so she peeked around Colonel Thomas' arm a few times instead. He had an array of bandages on his body, and he was sitting halfway up in the bed.

"We've cleaned and dressed his wounds as well as taken some skin from his back to place on his arms and legs where he was burned. He also has in a catheter so we can monitor the fluid resuscitation in his urine output. We'll continue to monitor his fluid balance and nutrition to make sure he's healing properly before we move him from HDU. Morphine will be given to him around the clock for pain, because it's going to be a bit extreme when he wakes up."

"What about his leg?"

"It's been operated on a little more just below his knee. We cleaned the damage up as much as we could, being that it was already detached due to the explosion. He may experience an imaginary pain that we call phantom limb pain." He looked at Lay-Lay as he spoke. "He'll feel pain where his leg is supposed to be. I know it's weird, but it's a common side effect."

Lay-Lay nodded her head and moved around him so that she could see Kyle fully. His eyes were closed, and his upper body was covered with the blanket and bandages. Her eyes traveled down the bed and landed on his legs. Where his leg had been removed was very visible. All she could see beneath the blanket was his knee. It went no further than that. It was a little larger than the other one, assumingly from bandages and swelling. More tears flowed as she made her way around the bed and sat in the chair next to his bed. She leaned forward and grabbed his hand. The size difference was evident as she laced their fingers together. His large hand enveloped hers loosely.

Lay had been waiting to be this close to him for so long that it felt unreal. She'd missed him terribly as the months passed, and she was finally back where she wanted to be. As Colonel Thomas exited discreetly, Lay-Lay kissed Kyle's hand over and over. She rubbed her hand lightly across his stomach as she stood to kiss his lips. One side of his face was covered with gauze, so she kissed the part that was exposed.

"I love you baby. I love you so much. I was scared you wasn't coming home to me...I missed you bae," she cried into his ear. Her face was nuzzled into the space between his neck and ear. She kept it there, inhaling his scent. After kissing down his neck, she sat back in the chair and grabbed his hand again and kissed it. She was so happy to see him that she couldn't stop kissing him. With her head lying on the bed next to where their hands were, she dozed off. She had been running since earlier that morning before class, and she was exhausted.

It had been a few hours by the time she woke up. She stirred around for a second before checking the clock on her cell phone.

"It's about time. I thought you and your man was going to sleep the day away," Hannah's voice startled her. She was standing in the corner of the room next to Arlington. They smiled at her as she stretched. She turned around to find Kyle still sleeping.

"How long have you guys been here?"

Arlington checked his watch. "For about an hour."

"Did they tell y'all about his umm..." Lay-Lay nodded her head towards his leg.

They both nodded their heads as Hannah began to cry again, which only made Lay-Lay cry again too. She looked down at his leg again, and ran her hand along his thigh. How in the hell was she supposed to tell Kyle that his leg was gone?

Chapter 7

"I said I'm fine!" Kyle yelled at the dietician as she gathered her things and left the room.

Lay-Lay shook her head at him. "You did not have to talk to her like that."

Kyle looked at her, sucked his teeth, and shrugged his shoulders. He had been acting like such a butthole since finding out his leg was gone. She had told him a few days ago when he woke up, and he still had the same little attitude.

"Kyle, people aren't going to continue to just let you talk to them any kind of way. I understand you're upset, but you could be a little nicer."

"You understand? Tell me Shalaya, just how in the hell would you understand when you still have both of your fucking legs?"

Lay-Lay looked at Kyle for a minute, trying to calm herself down. She didn't know who Kyle thought he was yelling at. She had been taking his rude ass remarks for the last couple of days like a champ, but this shit was starting to get on her nerves. If the situation had been any different, he would have gotten fucked up a long time ago. Crossing her arms over her chest, Lay-Lay shifted in her seat and stared at him.

"Fuck you looking at?"

"I'm looking at your ugly ass."

"If you got a problem with the way I treat people, then you can leave too."

This got Lay-Lay's attention. Never, in all the years she'd known him, had he talked to her like that. They'd gotten into it a few times, but he never spoke to her this harsh. It hurt her feelings to hear him talking to her like that, but she had a trick for him, because she wasn't the one.

"Listen here Kyle, clearly you're mad about the loss of your leg, and that's cool. You're entitled to that, but somewhere along the way you must have lost your fucking mind too. I am not the muthafucking one. If you want to bark out orders, I would advise you to call some of your soldiers up here and yell at their young asses. Get fucked up talking to me like that."

"Man Shalaya, go ahead with all that noise, I really ain't trying to hear it."

"Oh you don't want to hear it?"

Kyle pulled his covers up to his stomach and looked at her. "Nope."

"Cool." Lay-Lay grabbed her purse, keys, phone, and headed for the door. Kyle had her fucked all the way up.

She could understand that getting used to his condition was going to take some time, but she wasn't about to take the backlash for it. She had been more than sympathetic with his loss, but he was taking things to a totally different level. He'd been screaming at everybody that had come to see him. He down right refused for Morgan and Jade to come in. He went on and on about them not seeing his leg, like that mattered to anybody. Lay-Lay shook her head as she thought about how upset Morgan had been when he told the nurses not to let her in. That was messed up. She had driven all that way just for him to act crazy. They stayed for two more days, trying to get him to come around; when he didn't, Arlington suggested that they all go home and give him some time to heal. Of course, King and Dallas agreed. They made it very clear they weren't about to kiss Kyle's butt. Pulling out her phone, Lay-Lay called Morgan. She answered on the third ring.

Lay-Lay pressed the unlock button on Kyle's key fob. "Hey boo, you okay?"

"Yeah I'm good. How's Kyle?" The worry in Morgan's voice was evident.

"He's gon' be knocked the fuck out if he don't get his life together."

Morgan laughed for a few minutes. "Man Lay-Lay, you stupid. He must be still acting crazy?"

"Morgan, you have no idea. He's been yelling at everybody that comes in that musty ass room. The nigga ought to be glad those people will even come in there to check on his stinking self."

"Please tell me that nigga dun' took a shower."

"Nope. I guess he don't want people to see that lil nub." She and Morgan snickered at that a little before she continued. "But shit, he might as well let that lil bit right there go. That leg is a part of his life now. I mean, I know it's going to take him some time, but he's got to start acting better than this." Lay-Lay backed Kyle's truck out of the parking space and left the parking lot.

"Lay-Lay, you have to make him act right. He works at that hospital, don't let him embarrass himself. Please."

"I swear I'm trying, but you know that nigga had the nerve to tell me if I didn't want to hear his mouth then I could leave too?"

Morgan gasped. "Shut up Shalaya. No he didn't. Well what did you do?"

"What you think I did? I grabbed my stuff and left. I'm on my way home. I don't have time for Kyle's little tantrum. I'ma give him a few hours to get his mind right."

Lay-Lay and Morgan talked until Lay-Lay had gotten home and cooked. They'd even called Jade on three way while Lay-Lay cleaned up and did her and Kyle's laundry. By the time she'd finished, three hours had passed and she needed to shower. She told her girls she'd call them later and ended their call. Talking to her sisters had made her feel better. Stressed would be an understatement for the way she'd been feeling since Kyle had been in the hospital. Before she got into the shower, she turned her music all the way up and grabbed her body wash. She sang loudly as she scrubbed her body and washed her hair. When she got out, she put her Shea Moisture conditioner in her hair and combed through her curls. She wasn't really in the mood to straighten it right now, so she left it curly. Wrapped in her large, yellow terry cloth towel, she went into the room she now shared with him and grabbed a pair of black yoga pants, and the black long-sleeved Wounded Warrior shirt she'd gotten from the FRG over Kyle's battalion. She wasn't a big fan of the FRG (Family Readiness Group), because she felt like they were a bunch of lonely, messy wives, but they'd been a big help since Kyle had been back. Different girls stopped by the hospital to check on her every day. They either brought her food, coffee, or books to read. She'd learned about the things they did from the spouses group she was a part of on Facebook. She was actually grateful for them, although she wasn't much of a people person.

After putting on lotion and body spray, she grabbed her backpack from the closet and put her a change of clothes, her Kindle, and some conditioner into it. She went into her top drawer and grabbed her a pair of extra socks, and her headscarf as well. Once she was done gathering her things, she grabbed Kyle a few pair of gym shorts, the pack of white V-neck shirts she'd bought earlier, and all of his toiletries. She was making him bathe when she got back to that hospital, whether he wanted to or not. He was about to stop his foolishness. She looked around for his brush and shaving kit before throwing those things into her bag as well. When she was satisfied, she brushed her teeth, washed her face, grabbed her bag, and went to turn the music off. Scanning the house and making sure everything was in place, she noticed her charger still in the wall, so she grabbed that and made her way out of the door.

The ride to the hospital was a peaceful one. It was nearing eight o' clock at night, so it was already dark outside. She parked his truck in his usual spot and headed into the hospital. She spoke to the attendant at the front desk and headed for the elevator. When the doors opened, she was shocked to see Alissa in the corner. Lay-Lay gave her the once over before stepping on and pressing the number for Kyle's floor. She stood with her backpack on and her arms folded across her chest, waiting for the elevator.

"How is he doing?" Alissa's voice came out a lot nicer than it normally did.

I know she ain't trying to talk to me? Lay-Lay looked over her shoulder at Alissa quickly before turning back around. She started not to answer her, but changed her mind. If Alissa wanted to play nice, then she could too.

"Fine."

"They said he's being really rude to people. I tried to go up and see him today, but he wasn't taking visitors."

"He's not." Lay-Lay's voice was dry.

"Well if you know that, then why are you going?"

I knew this bitch was trying to be slick. Lay-Lay turned around and looked at Alissa. Her face decked a scowl as she looked Lay-Lay up and down.

"Bitch, you must think I'm you? I'm not just some random person he can turn down. He may have an attitude, but you think I care about that shit? No. I don't. I'm his fucking wife," Lay-Lay flashed the massive rock on her finger. "You better believe that nigga won't ever refuse a visit from me." Lay-Lay smirked at the look on Alissa's face and got off the elevator. It had just stopped on her floor. She looked back at Alissa once more and laughed before continuing down the hallway. Alissa had life fucked up if she thought she and Lay-Lay were in the same category when it came to Kyle.

"Good evening Mrs. Taylor. You're looking beautiful as always," the male nurse at the counter said.

"Thank you, sweetheart. How are you today?"

"Good. Let us know if you need anything." He walked around the station and headed down the hall in the opposite direction.

Lay-Lay said she would, and continued to Kyle's room. When she walked into the room, he was sitting straight up in the bed in the dark. There were no lights on, and the TV was turned off. The only lighting in the room came from the various monitors he was hooked up to. He had the curtains closed so tight you couldn't even see the lights from outside.

"Why you sitting in the dark, babe?" He looked over at her, but didn't say anything.

"Well, you being quiet is a lot better than you yelling at me. So I guess I'll take that." Lay-Lay put her backpack in the chair and slid the door to his room closed.

Once she flipped the lights on, his eyes squinted but he still didn't say anything. *Oh damn, he sexy when he mad.* His broad chest was halfway exposed due to the hospital gown having fell off his shoulder. Lay-Lay busied herself trying to clean his room. There were empty food containers and water bottles near his bed, along with flowers and balloons everywhere. His room was packed to the max with gifts from different people and places in the military. She sat all of the balloons and large flowers in the back of his room, while she placed the smaller ones on the windowsill. When she was finished, she stood at the foot of his bed with her hands on her hips.

"You ready to take a shower?"

"No. I'm not taking one."

"Oh yes you are. If you think you're about to keep sitting your butt in here stinking up these people's hospital room, you're so wrong."

Kyle let out a loud breath, but didn't say anything. Lay-Lay walked around to the side of his bed and pulled at the cover he had covering his lower body.

He snatched it away immediately. "Man, take your ass on Shalaya."

Lay-Lay grabbed a hand full of the cover again and pulled it. "Kyle, stop playing. You need to take a bath. You smell ridiculous." She pulled at the blanket again, only to have him pull it back. They participated in a full out tug of war for a few minutes before she was able to pull it away. With his face and arms still being in pain from the burns, he couldn't put up too much of a fight.

"Fuck Shalaya! Why you doing this shit?" Kyle's voice was so loud she jumped.

Lay-Lay stood still, not knowing what to say. She looked at him, and the way his chest heaved up and down as he breathed. His eyes looked evil, and his nostrils were flaring. She could tell he was angry, but by the way his voice cracked at the end of his sentence, she could also tell he was hurt. Lay-Lay's eyes trailed from his face down his body to his legs. The bandage just below his right knee was fresh and wrapped tightly.

"Why the fuck you staring at the shit? Give me back the blanket and get out, Shalaya." Kyle's head was still facing the door. He was talking, but he wasn't looking at her.

Lay-Lay stood, lost for a moment before going around to the other side of the bed so she could see his face. When she came around, he turned his head the other way, which was a very childish thing to do.

"Kyle, please stop it baby. Don't do this. Let me help you." She grabbed the bottom of his face trying to turn his head, but he wouldn't budge. "I love you babe, and I'm not leaving, so you might as well stop trying to push me away."

Lay-Lay sat there for a few minutes waiting on him to say something, but he didn't. She got up from the bed and kicked her flip-flops off. She went to the door and walked out. She informed the nurses station that she was about to help him shower, and asked if they could give them some privacy. Being that he wasn't their ordinary patient, they allowed this and told her to just call if she needed any assistance. When she got back, she slid the curtain over the glass door to his room and removed her pants and shirt. In nothing but her panties and bra, she walked into the bathroom and flipped the shower on. When she got back into the room, Kyle had turned around and was looking at her. His eyes roamed over her body as she walked towards him. No matter how mad or hurt he was, the lust in his eyes for her seeped through.

Lay-Lay stopped on the side of his bed. "See something you like?"

"Nah,"

Lay-Lay laughed before running her hand up his hardening length and stroking it. "You might not, but my little friend does."

Kyle grunted and tried to shift in his bed some. Lay-Lay wasn't letting up though. If sex would make him move, then that's what she'd use.

Lay-Lay kissed the side of his mouth. "Come on bae. Let's take a shower."

"I can't,"

"Why not?"

"I can't fucking walk, Shalaya," his voice boomed once again. In that short instant, he was back angry.

"I can help you, Kyle. We'll use the wheel chair and whatever you need help with, I'll help. You were there for me bae, let me be here for you," Lay-Lay rubbed the stubble growing along his jaw line. He hadn't shaved in a few days, and she was loving it. Normally his face was bare due to his job. "Please baby."

Lay-Lay could tell he was thinking about it, because he kept looking from her to the bathroom. When she stood up, she grabbed his hands and pulled lightly. He turned his head to face her, but still didn't move. Sensing his hesitation, she went to get the wheelchair and pushed it as close to the bed as she could get it.

"Ready babe?" Lay-Lay raised her brow as she held on to the wheelchair handles. When he nodded his head, she began jumping up and down while clapping her hands. "Yay! Lean all your weight on me if you need to. I'm strong, I can carry you."

Kyle chuckled lightly, and Lay-Lay thought she would melt. She'd been longing to see that beautiful smile for months.

Lay-Lay fanned her face dramatically. "Lawd, you so fine!"

Kyle's smile disappeared, and was replaced by a melancholy look. "I'm ready," was all he said as he scooted to the edge of the bed the best he could. Lay-Lay didn't miss the way his mood changed upon hearing her compliment, but she'd worry about that later. His arms were still very sore from the burns, so Lay-Lay made sure to help pull him the rest of the way.

Lay-Lay wrapped her arms around Kyle's waist as he used the bed railing to stand up. He wobbled a little as he tried to balance his weight on one foot. Lay-Lay held on tightly to him to make sure he didn't fall.

She eased back a little so he would have more space to move around, but didn't release him from her grip. He had a death grip on the bed railing, but he was doing well. The wobbling had almost stopped, and he was standing tall. He was looking straight ahead as he tried to focus on steadying himself.

"You're doing so good, baby. You wanna try to get to the wheelchair?" Lay-Lay released one arm from his waist and held him with one arm, with one of his arms draped over her shoulder for support. He was so much taller than her, so her head was practically under his armpit.

"Yeah, pull it closer." Kyle looked at the chair but didn't move.

Lay-Lay pulled it closer with her free hand and pushed the lock on the back of the wheel so it wouldn't move. When she was sure they were ready, she took a step forward, and he followed. Lay-Lay didn't know what went wrong, but they'd messed up somewhere along the way, and Kyle lost his balance. They both stumbled and swung in all types of directions, trying to gain their footing, but failed. Kyle fell first, hitting the wheelchair before slamming onto the hard floor, with Lay-Lay right behind him. They both screamed when she fell on top of him. Hers was a little louder than his, but his was laced with a great deal of pain. Lay scrambled to her feet trying to get off him but he wrapped both of his arms around her, stopping her movement.

"Stay right here mama, you're fine." His eyes were squeezed tightly shut. It was obvious he was in pain.

"You sure, Kyle? You look like you're in pain,"

"I just want to hold you for a minute."

"Can you hold me on the bed? This floor is cold."

Kyle's chest started to shake, causing Lay-Lay to look up at him. When she did, her heart warmed. He was laughing, and all she could see was the smile she loved so much.

"You're so crazy, Shalaya. I don't know where you come up with the shit you say."

Just as she was about to say something, his room door slid open and in walked two nurses, one being the male nurse she had just spoken to when she'd first gotten to the hospital. The other was a short, dark-haired girl that came in to change Kyle's bandages a few times. Lay-Lay looked at the floor in embarrassment.

"What happened?" the male nurse asked as he helped Kyle from the floor.

"I was trying to make his nasty ass take a shower and we fell," Lay-Lay wrapped the sheet from the bed around her body. She was still in her panties and bra from earlier.

Both nurses laughed as the brown -haired girl explained to Kyle that he was going to have to learn to rest all of his weight on his left leg, or he would lose his balance and fall every time. When she noticed the pitiful look on his face, she begged him not to feel bad because it was a common mistake made by newly amputated patients. When she was finished and Kyle was situated in the wheel chair, they left. Lay-Lay burst out laughing the moment they were gone. Kyle watched her for a long time before he too began to laugh.

"Can you imagine how stupid we must have looked laying on the floor?"

Kyle shrugged his shoulders "I don't give a fuck."

"Come on silly boy, let's take a shower. I'm sure the water probably cold by now." Lay-Lay pushed Kyle into the small restroom. It was a good thing there was a bench in the shower. She wasn't sure if they would be able to stand for too long. She didn't need a replay of their first fall.

*****

Helpless and horny. Those were the two things Kyle was feeling as he watched Lay-Lay sleep. She was curled up next to him in his bed. Her curly red hair was pulled up into a tight bun at the top of her head with the burgundy and black rose scarf wrapped around her head. She was dressed lightly in panties and one of his tank tops. Kyle ran his finger across the tiny brown freckles that decorated the bridge of her nose and under her eyes.

Freckles was one of the many things he loved about her face. Kyle was trying his hardest to keep his composure because of where they were, but Lay-Lay was making that hard. Every time she moved or inhaled deeply, her breasts moved.

As if that wasn't enough, she had kicked one leg from beneath the cover, giving him the perfect view of her butt in her little purple panties. He'd been looking at the TV for the last few minutes, because he couldn't sleep. However, his eyes continued to travel to her body. He'd been missing her and the way her warmth always seemed to envelope him perfectly. When they were in the shower earlier, he'd almost lost his mind as she bathed him. If the water hadn't been extremely painful against his raw arms, he probably would have tried his luck. The excruciating pain cut that short. He was in and out in less than five minutes. Kyle looked down at his leg. He'd pulled the blanket from it so he could look at it.

This shit was messing with his mental. Never in his entire life had he ever been this helpless and dependent on someone else. He had to hurry and heal so he could get a prosthetic. He refused to let this beat him. Lay-Lay shifted in the bed, throwing her hand above her head and jolting him from his thoughts. Her pretty face was scrunched into a small frown with her lips poked out. *I gotta get right for my baby.* Kyle observed her features for a little longer as he thought about their life together.

It was clear she wasn't giving up on him. The entire ride from Germany to South Carolina, she'd been the only thing on his mind. He hadn't known the extent of his injuries, but her face was all he could think about. Her smile, her heart, and the way she loved him was something to come home to. When he opened his eyes after his surgery and saw her sleeping with her head lying on his bed, he thought his life was perfect. There was nothing more he could have asked for.

"Get some rest babe," Lay-Lay's voice was soft and groggy as she snuggled closer to him.

He smiled at how she kept scooting closer to him. It was almost as if she couldn't get close enough.

"Get up and show me some love, Shalaya." He watched her lay still for a few more minutes before sliding from beneath the covers and straddling his lap.

"Am I hurting you?" She leaned forward and lay her head on his chest, with her arms halfway around his waist.

"Nah mama, you good. I love you."

"I love you too Kyle. More than anything. Thank you for coming back to me. If you hadn't, I probably would have lost my mind."

"I'll always come home to you, Shalaya," Kyle rubbed his hands up and down her back. "You know something, when that building blew up and we were waiting on help, you were all I could think about. I kept asking God to let me make it back for you. I could hear your voice as I pictured your pretty face. I was daydreaming about you so hard, it was like I could feel you next to me. It was only then that I closed my eyes and relaxed my body. I prayed to God until I lost consciousness. I prayed about everything. My life, my job, you and our love, my parents, my sister and the babies…everything." Kyle's voice trailed off.

"When I got that phone call from Captain Long, I just fell out. I was at school and I hit the ground in front of everybody. You should have saw me bae, I couldn't move. Just the thought of you leaving me had me paralyzed for a minute," Lay-Lay leaned back and rubbed his shoulders, and kissed his lips. "If you had died, I was serious about losing my mind. I don't know if I would have been able to go on, babe. I love you. Sometimes I feel like you're all I have," Lay-Lay began to cry.

Kyle wiped her tears and pulled her back to his chest. "Need God, the way you need me, Shalaya. Whether I'm here or not, He will be. I felt a sense of comfort as I prayed when I was out there. I knew no matter what happened, we would be all right because it would have been His will."

"But who would have been my husband then?"

She joined in on his laughter as he held her close. She scooted her bottom closer to his stomach, which caused her warmth to rub across his already hardening wood. His breath got ragged as she continued to grind subtly in his lap. He gripped her ass, positioning her right on his hard length.

"You trying to show your man some love for real, huh?"

"You know me baby. I don't know why you playing. I been waiting on you to take a shower so I could get me a little bit."

Kyle squeezed a handful of her ass and planted kisses all over her face. He kissed her lips before trailing down to her neck. He swirled his tongue around her neck, stopping every few seconds to suck on it. He left a light red mark on every area his tongue grazed. Her moans had him ready to throw her down on the bed and dick her down something serious, but his current condition was preventing that.

"Lift up bae, and put him in," Kyle's hooded eyes observed her lightly flushed face as she lifted up on her legs. He reached down and slid her panties to the side so she could slide down onto him. He could feel her juices on the head of his dick as she glided it around in her essence before sliding down onto it.

"Ahhhhh shit...fuck...ummm damn Shalaya," Kyle mumbled a little of everything. She was so tight and warm. Her body was the perfect fit for his. The way her wet walls pulled him in every time she slid up and down had his toes curling. She was moaning like crazy, making his dick even harder, if that was even possible. He bit her shoulder as she slowed down and moved her hips in a circle. "This shit right here is why daddy was missing home."

Kyle pushed his hips up towards her while holding onto her hips. Before long, he could feel himself nearing an orgasm.

"I'm finna cum bae," Kyle bit her nipple softly through her shirt.

"No wait, I want to cum with you baby. Can I cum too Kyle, please? Please daddy?" Lay-Lay's forehead was pressed against his shoulder as she moaned incoherently. She was so caught up in the moment; she was begging for something he was going to give her anyway. He slapped her butt, causing her to speed up. "Don't get lazy Shalaya, ride this dick baby. It's yours."

Lay-Lay began bouncing and moving around on Kyle's dick as he held onto her sides. His bottom lip was tucked between his teeth as he watched her move. Her scarf had fallen off her head, exposing her curly hair. Kyle reached up and pulled the band from her ponytail, letting it fall.

"You're sexy as fuck with this curly ass hair." Kyle ran his fingers through it as he watched her face change. When he felt her thighs tighten against his, he knew she was close to climaxing. "Don't hold back, baby. Let me feel it."

"Ummmmm Kyle. Baby!" she squealed as she creamed all over his dick.

When Kyle looked down and saw her essence coating his dick, he couldn't hold it anymore and bust inside of her. She fell forward and rested her head against his shoulder. He wrapped his arms tightly around her, just enjoying the feel of her body next to his. He kissed her ear before telling her to get something for them to clean up with. She slowly pulled them apart and went to the restroom, and returned with a warm soapy washcloth. When she was done washing them, she changed her panties and T-shirt.

She looked at him while dressing. "Babe, you know that song by Aloe Blacc called "The Man"?"

Kyle looked at her skeptically before nodding his head yes.

"That should be your theme song. Whenever you walk into a room it should automatically start playing."

Kyle shook his head and laughed at her. This girl was a fucking character. She kept him laughing.

"I'm serious bae. You the man. I'm standing here looking at you and all I can hear is that song playing in my head. It ain't even just the sex either, you're just the man period. Yeah, you can tell everybody, go ahead and tell everybody, you the man, you the man, you the man, yes you are, yes you are, yes you are," Lay-Lay danced around in a circle as she sang to Kyle.

He watched her standing in his hospital room singing and dancing in her T-shirt and panties, looking like she didn't have a care in the world. Her face was bright, and her smile was glowing. Not one time had she acted weirded out by his injuries. Instead, she embraced it. Even with one leg, and over forty percent of his body covered in second-degree burns, he felt like the happiest man alive. Kyle felt like a bitch as he sat there watching her in awe. Everything about her had him in love. Shalaya was his muthafucking baby!

Chapter 8

"Kyle, hurry up babe."

Kyle licked his tongue up the center of her back before kissing the back of her neck. Lay-Lay's body shivered continuously as he slid in and out of her. She looked back over her shoulder at him before rubbing her hand across his exposed stomach. Her eyes were filled with lust as she moaned her appreciation to him. Kyle and Lay-Lay held eye contact, staring each other down until Kyle leaned down closer to her with his chest pressed against her back.

Lay-Lay gasped loudly as she felt his dick in her stomach. "Come on babe, give me more. Aw...shit! Harder baby...go harder!"

Kyle knew she would get with the program once he started hitting her with that grown man dick. He hadn't been able to give it to her right since he'd been home. Kyle lifted up some so he could watch her ass jiggle.

"Fuck mama!" Kyle's voice came out as more of a whine than anything.

Lay-Lay's eyes shot open with alarm. "What baby? Are you in pain?"

Kyle's body tensed as he tried to hold out from busting so early. He shook his head from side to side with his mouth hanging halfway open, and his eyes closed. He slammed his pelvis gently into her, trying to grind deeper.

"Kyle!"

"Shit baby, umm...aw damn Shalaya!" Kyle's breathing picked up drastically as he became engrossed in ecstasy. Kyle and Lay-Lay were so caught up in each other, that they didn't hear the door open until it was too late.

"Y'all so damn nasty!" Jade's voice caught them both by surprise.

"Oh shit!" Kyle stopped moving and just held on to Lay-Lay's waist, looking like a deer caught in headlights.

"Babe, why you stop? It's only Jade's ass, she ain't nobody."

Kyle snickered a little. "Shalaya?"

"What? She can watch–hell, I don't care. Just keep fucking me!"

Jade and Kyle both laughed as she headed back out the door. "I'll make sure nobody else comes in. Y'all just hurry y'all nasty asses up." Jade closed the door.

"You so wild, Shalaya," Kyle began moving again, this time a lot harder and faster. He needed to hurry and finish before someone else came in. He and

Lay-Lay were in the middle of his hospital room fucking like they were at home. "Shit baby, I'm finna bust."

Lay-Lay moaned as she repeatedly threw her ass back, trying to match his pace. A few strokes later, they were both cumming with a loud moan escaping her lips. She lie on the bed face down for a few seconds, until he lifted her up and pushed her towards the bathroom. She returned, cleaned them both up, and fixed her clothing before helping him with his. It had been three weeks since his surgery, and his leg was finally healed enough for him to get fitted for his prosthetic leg.

He'd been going to physical therapy for the past few weeks, and he was now more mobile and doing a lot more things on his own. He watched Lay-Lay walk to the door and open it for Jade once they were situated. He looked down, trying to hide his smile when she walked in. She had her arms folded across her chest, looking from him to Lay-Lay.

"Y'all are two of the nastiest people I've ever met in my life. Kyle, I expected this kind of mess from Lay-Lay, but not you. You're letting her pervert you." Jade's tone was a mix of accusing and humorous.

Lay-Lay walked from the mirror and sat on the bed next to Kyle. "Girl, don't let Kyle fool you. It was his idea. This nigga is just as nasty as me. I thought I had it bad, but I ain't got nothing on my baby. He be having your girl filled up."

"TMI bitch, TMI!" Jade covered her ears playfully.

Kyle pulled Lay-Lay closer to him and kissed her neck. "What you doing back up here, I thought y'all were heading back out this morning?"

"We were, but I forgot my baby's pack and play at y'all house. I needed to get the keys."

"I'll take y'all back to the house. Kyle has to get ready for his fitting anyway." Lay-Lay hopped of the bed, grabbed her things, and left behind Jade.

Once the girls were gone, Kyle tried to fix his blankets the best he could. He didn't need the prosthetic provider getting a whiff of what he'd been up to while awaiting his arrival. He and Lay-Lay had just changed the compression stocking he was wearing before she bent over in her little skirt, making his dick hard. It had been a done deal after that. She knew what she was doing wearing that little shit up there in the first place. Scooting back on his bed, Kyle flipped the TV on and flipped through the channels. Since there was nothing really on, he used this time to think and pray.

He thanked God for allowing his family to understand the things he was going through, and giving him time to get over it. In the beginning, he had been a complete jerk to them all, but they stayed. They had even traveled back down earlier this week to check in on his progress. Morgan, Dallas, the twins, King, Jade, baby Kingston, and his parents had been staying at his house and visiting him every day this week. Of course, Lay-Lay was back and forth between his house and the hospital, making sure everyone was comfortable. He had to fight her tooth and nail every night to make her sleep at home with everyone else.

Although he would have liked for her to sleep at the hospital with him like she'd been doing, he didn't think that was a good idea right now. He hadn't told her, but he'd been having some of the worst nightmares for the past few days. They hadn't been there in the beginning, but for some reason now whenever he would close his eyes, he would visualize the war zone and the things that had taken place there. He hadn't told anyone, because this happened every time he came home from deployments.

"Good evening, Major Taylor." Kyle looked to the door and noticed the prosthesis provider had come in.

"You ready to get started?" He pulled his bag from his shoulder and pulled up a chair next to Kyle's bed.

"Yes sir. Let's get it done."

*****

Sporadic movements thumped against his hand every so often as he lie awake staring at the ceiling.

It was going on three in the morning, and Smoke hadn't been to sleep yet. Kristen and Caleb had gone to bed early, leaving him and Cailyn awake. Smoke had placed his hand over Kristen's stomach a few seconds ago when he noticed the baby's kicks.

"You gon' be up keeping daddy company, huh baby girl?" Smoke rubbed Kristen's stomach some more before rolling over.

It had been almost two months since Lay-Lay had moved to South Carolina with that nigga, and even longer since he'd been apart from her. He hadn't known missing Lay-Lay would be this hard. She had spoiled him by taking him back fast in the past. Now he expected that same treatment every time. This time was proving to be different. Every day, he woke up with her on his mind. Although being at the house with Kristen and Caleb full time was making her being gone easier to deal with, it still wasn't the same. Lay-Lay had been a major factor in his life for so many years that it felt impossible to live without her.

"Why you still up?" Kristen rolled over and laid her head on his bare chest.

Smoke wrapped his arm around her, pulling her closer to his body. "Can't sleep."

"What's on your mind?"

"Ain't shit really. Just life."

Kristen ran her hand across his stomach just as his phone vibrated. Smoke looked over to the nightstand and held his breath. Kristen was about to go ham. He waited a little bit longer, praying for it to stop but God must couldn't have been paying him any attention, because it didn't.

"So you ain't gon' get your phone?" She sat up and looked at him.

"Nah it's cool. Lay back down."

Kristen got up and snatched it from the dresser before he could say anything else. He started to hop up and take it from her, but changed his mind. Shit, if she wanted to hurt her own feelings, then that was her business.

"Who the fuck is Emoni?"

Ah Shit, Moni. Smoke had to hold in his smile. She was a bad little female he'd met at work a few days ago. He'd cut her son's hair on Tuesday and fucked her on Wednesday. Her pussy was A-fucking-one, and he didn't see himself leaving her alone any time soon.

Kristen threw Smoke's phone and hit him in the face. "I said who the fuck is Emoni, Smoke?"

"Kris, you better lay your ass back down and shut the fuck up talking to me. I ain't tell your ass to grab my shit. That's what you get."

Smoke laid back down, preparing to go to sleep when his phone rang again. He sucked his teeth when he read Lana's name. *Why all these hoes up so late?* He ignored her call and powered his phone off. He could feel Kristen's gaze on him, but he wasn't in the mood for her shit tonight.

"Smoke, get up and get your shit and get out of my house."

"Kristen, you must be out your fucking mind. You better lay your ass back down and got to sleep."

"No Smoke, I'm serious. Please just leave. I asked you good before you started staying over here again were you ready and you said yes. Clearly you're not, so leave."

Smoke turned back over so he could see her face. He was surprised to see how serious she looked. Her face was calm and her arms were folded beneath her breasts. She raised one eyebrow at him as he looked her over. Apparently, he wasn't moving fast enough for her because she started moving around the room, snatching his things and throwing them into a pile in the middle of the floor.

"What the fuck you doing? Girl, lay your ass down!" Smoke got up and stepped into her face.

"I'll lay down after you leave." She sat down on the bed and watched him.

"You serious?"

"Hell yeah I'm serious. I'm not about to keep taking this shit from you, Smoke. Lay-Lay got smart enough and left your ass, and I have no problem doing the same. You almost ran that damn girl crazy. You got me fucked up if you think I'ma stick around and let you do the same shit to me."

The mention of Lay-Lay's name made Smoke's temper flare. He didn't have to take this shit from Kristen. He'd been fucking around on her since they'd first gotten together; now all of a sudden, since Lay-Lay wanted to grow a fucking backbone, Kristen wanted to play follow the leader. *Fuck her!* Smoke grabbed his things from the floor and threw them back into the closet. He'd be back to get that shit later. Kristen never stayed mad long. She was actually surprising him, though. After throwing his things into the closet, she should have been changing her mind, but she hadn't. She was still in the same spot, with the same ugly ass frown on her face.

"So I guess since my main bitch left me, all my side hoes gon' fall in line behind her, huh? It's just fuck Smoke now, right? Well you know what…fuck you and the other bitches too."

Smoke threw his hoodie on, grabbed his phone and keys, and left. He made sure to slam the door on the way out. Once he got outside, he looked up towards the window and he could see her watching him. She looked sad, but shit, this was her fault. The sight of her round stomach poking out of her shirt almost changed his mind, but instead of going back into the house like he wanted to, he got in his truck and pulled off.

Kristen watched Smoke's truck back out of her driveway and finally let her tears fall. She'd been holding them in since she first picked up his phone and saw the girl's picture. She was pretty and it made Kristen's stomach ache. Thinking about the things she and Smoke did, and him doing it to another woman made her want to throw up. All she asked was for that nigga to do right, and he just refused to, so she refused to tolerate it. As much as it would hurt to do so, she had to leave Smoke alone. Heartache and pain was all too familiar in her life, simply because of him. She looked out of the window for a little while longer before heading back to bed. Tomorrow was a new day; she would be on the lookout for her kids' a new daddy.

*****

"Ahhhhhhh!!! NO! No! NO!" Kyle's screams startled Lay-Lay, breaking her from her sleep.

She looked over at him as he tossed and turned in his sleep. His fists were balled up tightly against his sides as he moved his head from side to side. She could hear him grinding his teeth as he released painful growls. She sat frozen for a second, just watching him. When he swung one of his arms, she jumped back so hard, that she fell to the floor. You would have thought the loud thump her body made as it slammed on the floor would have awakened him, but nope.

He was still in bed, writhing from his nightmare. Lay-Lay got off the floor and grabbed his shirt to shield her naked body. She stood back observing him for a moment before going around to his side of the bed. He'd been having nightmares for the past two months since he'd been home. Because it didn't happen every night, she hadn't bothered to mention it to him, but tonight was different. The sounds he was making had never been this bad before.

"Babe, wake up...Kyle, get up baby, you're having a nightmare," she shook his shoulder roughly, trying to pull him from the dark place he was in. "Kyle! Get up!"

His body jumped harshly before his eyes popped open. His gaze looked far away as he circled the room before stopping his line of vision on Lay-Lay. He scrunched his eyes up, as if trying to see if she was really there or not. After wiping his eyes with his hand, he closed them again and kept them closed.

Lay-Lay touched his chest, which was damp from sweat before climbing into bed beside him. "You okay?"

"Yea.,"

"What were you dreaming about?"

"Nothing."

Lay-Lay pinched his side. "Stop lying and tell me."

"My deployment."

"The explosion or everything?"

He cleared his throat. "Everything. My explosion mostly."

"Do you think you need to get some help for this?"

Kyle pushed her off of him and rolled over so he could get out of bed. Lay-Lay watched the muscles in his back flex as he limped into the bathroom. The prosthetic leg was growing on him, but he still walked with a slight limp. His physical therapist said it wouldn't be long before he was back to walking correctly. The limp and the fake leg didn't bother Lay-Lay either way.

Kyle, on the other hand, wasn't feeling it in the least. She listened as the water in the shower came on. *I know this nigga didn't?* He had gotten out of bed and completely disregarded her question. *Oh, he got me fucked up.* Lay-Lay slid off the bed and headed for the bathroom. She turned the knob, but the door was locked.

"Oh hell nah," Lay-Lay twisted the knob again, just to be sure it was locked and sure enough, it was. "Hell he think he is locking doors around here?"

Lay-Lay beat on the door hard with her fist. "Kyle, open up this damn door." She beat on it a few more times before she realized he wasn't about to open it. "I got something for him." She marched to the kitchen, checking the drawers and beneath the sink for something to unlock the door.

"I know he got some tools around here somewhere." She scoured the kitchen until she found a screwdriver. With motive and her screwdriver, she hightailed it right back to her bathroom. The water was still running, so she knew the coast was clear. She twiddled the lock with the screwdriver until she realized it wasn't budging.

"Dang man." She stood staring at the door, trying to figure out another way to get in, until she got an idea. She bent down so that she was eye level to the knob and began to screw the screws out of the door. It took her a few minutes, but she eventually got it. The knob to the door fell and hit the rug, barely missing her toes. "Yes!"

When she pushed the door open, steam invaded her space. He must have had that water on fire hot, because the heat encompassed her body immediately. She walked to the shower door and snatched it open. Kyle was sitting on the floor of the shower with his legs spread out in front of him. He scrambled to cover the stump of his leg with a towel, which only made him look like a fool because there was no way in hell he could cover his big leg with that small washcloth.

"Kyle, what the fuck are you doing? I can still see that shit." Lay-Lay stood in the door, letting the water sprinkle her face.

"Close the door Shalaya, you wetting up the floor.

"I wish I would close a fucking door. Me or you will not be closing nor will you be locking another damn door in this house. You know the kind of trouble I had to go through to get this door open all because you want to act silly." Lay-Lay was trying to lighten the mood, but he wasn't budging. "Do you hear me? You might as well move this lil shit," she snatched the washcloth from his leg before he had the time to stop her. "Because this is a part of our life now. I do not care about your leg, Kyle. When will you see that?"

Kyle leaned against the wall of the shower with his eyes locked on her. His anger was evident. Although he was trying to mask it, the aura was overpowering. "CLOSE THE FUCKING DOOR SHALAYA!"

"Fuck no." Lay-Lay removed her shirt and got into the shower with him. She closed the door and slid down onto the floor next to him. She sat quietly for a second, trying to ease the tension, but it wasn't working. Kyle was angry and he wasn't letting up. Lay-Lay was wracking her brain trying to think of something to say; when she couldn't think of anything, she slid closer to his leg and leaned down to kiss it. He jumped, almost kneeing her in the forehead. She moved back a little to give him some space so he could see what she was about to do. She lowered her head slower this time, until her lips met the bottom of his knee. She kissed all over it, trying to assure him that it didn't bother her.

When she looked up into his eyes, she could see the agony and discomfort but she continued. Clearly, not having a whole leg was still bothering him. They held eye contact as her lips traced the smooth skin of his healed injury. Her heart went out to him. This couldn't be easy, but at some point he was going to have to man up and deal with it. Once she removed her lips, she replaced it with her hand. It felt weird as hell as she rubbed it, but she wasn't stopping until he knew that her love was unconditional.

Lay-Lay rested her hand on his kneecap. "You have to get past this, Kyle." He sat still not saying anything, just looking straight ahead.

"Kyle, you are more than just this leg. It was sexy and all, but I can do without it, and so can you."

"That's easy for you to say because it's not you." Kyle's remark was a mix between anger and sarcasm.

"It is me. As long as you're my husband, whatever problems you have are mine too. Now if you don't feel the same way, then you should probably divorce me. I'm overbearing as hell, and you already know that."

Kyle finally looked at her. She smiled, but he didn't. "You're right. We probably should get a divorce. We moved too fast anyway."

Lay-Lay grabbed her chest, trying to catch her breath. Kyle's words were like a swift kick to the chest. Her eyes searched his frantically for anything that would tell her he was just playing but she saw nothing. His face was hard, like she'd never seen it before. His eyes were steady, and his mouth was flat.

"That's how you feel?"

"Yes."

"Well oh damn well, because I'm not giving you a divorce."

"Don't make this hard, Shalaya."

"I'm not making anything hard, you are."

"Our marriage was rushed. I only married you because I thought I was going to die. I didn't, so now you can leave."

Lay-Lay's throat got tight as she fought back tears. Her stomach did somersaults as she processed the things that were coming out of his mouth. She knew he was hurt, but she didn't know he felt like this. Unable to take the pain, Lay-Lay jumped up from the floor and ran from the bathroom. Once she was back in her room, she went into the closet and threw her clothes around until she located her jogging suit. She was in such a rush that she put it on with no undergarments.

Fully dressed, she walked back out of the closet and brushed her hair into a ponytail. She put her headscarf, cell phone, phone charger, and iPad into her large purse, and grabbed her keys. The shower water was still running, so she knew he was still in the bathroom sulking. Without grabbing another thing, Lay-Lay walked out of the bedroom she shared with him and down the stairs. Her school bag carrying her laptop and law books was sitting on the sofa. She threw that over her shoulder and exited the house. Although it was in the wee hours of the morning, she had to go. There was no way she could stay. With a broken heart for the second time, this one a lot worse than the first one, Lay-Lay got into her car and headed back to Atlanta.

Completely unaware of what was going on, Kyle sat in the shower in the same spot. His mind was all over the place, because he'd just done the last thing he'd ever wanted to do. Hurt his wife. Promising to love and to cherish Shalaya wasn't something he took lightly, but how could he do that in the state he was in? He felt like half of a man, and she deserved a whole one–s man that could protect her and love her fully, but he was no longer sure he could. He didn't even love himself anymore. Everything she said sounded good, but how long would that last? When would she get tired of looking at him limp around?

What would she do if a normal man that didn't have nightmares, or one that had both of his legs approached her? Could he trust her to stay true to him? These were the things that had been torturing him for the past couple of days. He couldn't help letting his feelings get the best of him. Kyle stayed in the shower until the water turned cold.

He tried to convince himself that he needed time to think, and that he hadn't stayed in there so long because he was afraid to face Shalaya. With a towel wrapped loosely around his waist, Kyle hopped from the restroom. He hadn't even bothered to put his prosthetic back on. He was shocked to see that she wasn't in bed. He looked around the room before moving to the closet. Nothing. He called her name, only for her not to answer. He called it again while walking to the edge of the staircase to look over the balcony. He sat on the stairs and slid down one by one, until he reached the bottom.

She was nowhere in sight. After checking all the rooms downstairs, Kyle slowly made his way to the window. When he peered outside, her car was gone. He cursed as he headed back for the stairs. Once he was upstairs, he grabbed his phone and called her. She sent him straight to the voicemail. He checked the clock. It was too early to call anybody, but he needed to check on her so he called Morgan. She didn't answer the first time, so he called back again. This time she picked up in a groggy voice.

"Hello."

"Sorry to wake you Morg, but have you talked to Shalaya?"

"No. What's wrong? Is everything okay?" The alarm in Morgan's voice was evident.

"We had a fight and she left."

Morgan sighed. "She probably just needed some fresh air, she'll be back."

"I don't know, Morgan. I told her I wanted a divorce."

"You told her what? HAVE YOU LOST YOUR MIND? You know what kind of mental state that damn girl is in? You want her to lose her fucking mind, Kyle?"

Morgan wasn't making him feel any better about what he'd done. He was so selfish he hadn't even been thinking of the way she might have taken this. All he thought about was himself.

"Kyle! Don't your ass get quiet now. I'll call you back in a minute; let me try to call this girl and see where she's at." Moran hung up without waiting for an answer.

Kyle felt bad about the way he'd handled things, but that didn't change his mind about the things he'd said. He could have found an easier way to tell her how he was feeling, but he didn't regret it one bit, because it was the truth. Defeated, he got into bed and waited for Morgan to call him back. Seconds turned into minutes, while minutes turned into hours. When he could no longer take it, he called Morgan back. He was caught off guard by the sound of Lay-Lay's voice. He pulled the phone back to make sure he'd dialed the right number. Morgan had merged him in on their call.

"Shalaya, where are you?"

"Morgan, I'ma kill your ass," Lay-Lay said as she realized Kyle was on the phone.

"Why'd you leave?" Silence.

"I'm sorry I yelled at you baby, I really am." Silence.

"Shalaya, please talk to me." Kyle's voice was desperate.

"Lay-Lay, please talk to him," Morgan chimed in.

"I'm on the highway headed home."

Kyle released a frustrated breath. "You can't go running back to Atlanta every time we have an argument. That's not how a marriage works."

"If I remember correctly you want a divorce, so it doesn't really matter how a marriage works, now does it?"

Kyle couldn't say anything to that, so he sat quiet.

"Exactly. Now get off of my phone. Morgan, I'll hit you back later boo." Shalaya hung up, leaving him and Morgan on the phone.

Morgan didn't say anything, but he knew his sister. She had an earful for him, but she was holding back. Kyle waited for her to say something, but she never did.

"What do I do now, Morgan?"

"I don't know big brother. Do you really believe the stuff that you told her?"

"Yeah."

"Well maybe you should get a divorce then. Goodnight. I love you."

Kyle's line went dead. Morgan was mad too. He closed his eyes and thought about getting in his truck to follow her back to Atlanta, but changed his mind. He wasn't comfortable enough driving with one leg yet and besides, they both needed some time to think.

Chapter 9

When Lay-Lay pulled into the parking lot of her apartment complex, she was too happy. She was extremely tired, and could only imagine how good her bed was about to feel. Thank God no one was in her parking spot. She pulled her car in, parked, and hurried up the stairs with the two bags she brought from South Carolina. It was clean, just like she'd left it. Everything felt right, except the fact that she had no business being there, at least not alone anyway. Tears clouded her eyes again. She had to have some type of curse on her or something, because she couldn't keep a man to save her life. No matter what she did, they always found a reason to leave. Salty water fell freely as she undressed and climbed in bed naked. As tired as she was, sleep didn't come so easy. Her mind was filled with thoughts of her and Kyle, followed by ones of her and Smoke. Those two niggas had taken her through the ringer; she needed to get a grip on life before she lost her sanity.

"Bitch, what's this I hear about you driving all the way back to Georgia in the middle of the damn night?" Jade asked as soon as Lay-Lay answered the phone.

She rolled over and looked at the clock on her dresser. She hadn't even known she had fallen to sleep until she'd just woke up. The last thing she remembered was crying about the two dogs in her life.

"That nigga made me mad."

"I can tell, but you crazy. Ain't no way in hell I would have driven nowhere that time of night. Mad or not, I would have waited 'til in the morning. King's ass would have just had to be mad."

Lay-Lay laughed. "I feel you, but I needed to get away from that nigga. My feelings were hurt, and I didn't trust myself. Morgan would hate me if I would have killed her brother last night."

Jade and Lay-Lay both burst out laughing. They both knew she was only joking, but it was funny as hell.

"Man Lay-Lay, you stupid. Get up so we can go get our nails and toes done."

"Now you know I just got in, I'm tired girl. I need a few more hours of sleep first."

"Sleep when you die. I'm finna go get Morgan, and we'll be over there in a minute."

Lay-Lay tossed her phone onto the bed and rolled back over. She fell right back to sleep with no problem. The only reason she ended up right back awake was because someone was beating on her door. She squinted her eyes as the sun shined through her windows. For a second she laid back down, and let whomever it was continue beating on her door. The longer they knocked, the harder they knocked, so she pulled herself from bed and wrapped her robe around her body.

She wasn't surprised to see Jade and Morgan standing at the door when she opened it. Her face was frowned up, but eased up a little when she saw Daylen's little bright eyes staring at her. Morgan had her hair in two little ponytails with bows on them. The bows practically covered the ponytails because she didn't have much hair, but it was still the cutest thing. When Lay-Lay stuck her hands out. she dove straight for her.

"Heyyyyy auntie baby!" Lay-Lay squealed as she backed up into the house. "I'm only letting y'all in because y'all got my babies with you."

Jade was holding baby King's carrier, as Morgan sat Tre down on the floor. He crawled right over to baby King's carrier and pulled up on it. Lay-Lay watched in awe at how much the twins had grown.

"Girl, go get dressed. Ain't nobody come over here for you to have no play date with the kids."

Lay-Lay frowned her face up at Morgan.

"You can shut up, because who in the hell brings all these damn babies to go to the nail salon anyway? What we bout to get accomplished?"

"We each can get a baby bitch, don't try to be funny. Since Daylen wants to hop her lil happy butt to you, she can be yours for the day. Now go put on your clothes so we can go," Morgan pushed Lay-Lay playfully.

Once she was in her room, Lay-Lay grabbed a black romper with some wedge sandals and put it on. She brushed her long red hair into a bun at the top of her head, handled her hygiene, and headed back to the front. They all piled in Jade's truck and left to get their day started.   The nail salon was packed as usual, but the girls managed to get in all together. They were seated in three chairs right next to each other, with a baby in their lap. Jade had just finished telling them about some of the kids from King's job when Morgan nudged her shoulder. She nodded her head towards the door, and Lay-Lay and Jade both turned their heads to see Sharia walking in. Jade had to laugh to herself, because she hadn't seen this hoe since she beat her ass in the trailer park.

"Ooh Jade, show her lil King. He cute as hell and look just like King. Go show him to her." Lay-Lay was always looking for a way to start some mess.

"I should, shouldn't I?"

Morgan sat up in her chair so that she could see both of them at the same time. "No you should not. We too old to be fighting. Plus, I ain't going to jail for cruelty to children. All these damn kids in this shop, they'll hurry up and lock us up."

Lay-Lay tooted her lips up and rolled her eyes. "You get on my nerves. Always ruining the fun for everybody else."

"Don't she though? Lil sour bitch make me sick," Jade agreed with Lay-Lay.

Their laughing drew a few stares from some of the people in the shop, including Sharia. When she saw them, she turned her head and pretended that she didn't. That was cool for the time being, but the little Chinese lady that was doing her feet sat her in the chair right next to Lay-Lay's loud mouth ass. Sharia was about to sit down when Lay-Lay tapped the shoulder of the lady that was about to do Sharia's feet.

"Can you sit her somewhere else? We don't like her."

Jade and Morgan both tried to suppress their laughter. Lay-Lay was showing slap out.

"She ain't got to sit me nowhere. I'm about to sit right here. I ain't worried about y'all," Sharia mugged all three of the women, stopping at Jade. Her eyes traveled down to the precious little dark baby that she held. Baby Kingston was wide awake, trying to hold his little head up. The dark hair that was on his head was lying down around his face, nearly touching his eyebrows. His dark gray onesie had Kingston wrote on the front of it in black letters. The way Sharia stared at him didn't go unnoticed by the girls, even though she caught herself and tried to turn her head.

Instead of saying anything, the three friends opted to turn around and finish enjoying their pedicures. When they were done, they put the babies in their strollers and walked down the rest of the strip mall. Since they were all hungry, they decided to stop at Red Robin and eat. It was a cute little burger joint that was never really too packed. Inside and seated at their booth, they finally addressed the matter at hand. Thankfully, all three of the babies had fallen asleep so they could have lunch in peace. Morgan asked first.

"So y'all getting a divorce for real or not?"

Lay-Lay shrugged her shoulders, and picked at the basket of seasoned fries. "I don't know. If that's what he really wants, then yeah."

"What you mean if that's what he wants? You know Kyle didn't mean that mess. He's just going through a lot right now," Morgan looked at Lay-Lay with sympathetic eyes.

"I can understand that, but I'm not about to make this man stay with me if he doesn't want to. I've tried everything I can to make sure he knows my love for him is real. If he chooses not to see it, I don't know what else I'm supposed to do."

Jade rubbed Lay-Lay's shoulder when she saw her eyes water. "Y'all need each other, Lay-Lay. He was there for you, so you have to be there for him. I know him pushing you away is hard, but take it. He doesn't mean any of this. Look at what he's going through. He might feel like you deserve better than him or something."

"That so crazy though. I don't care about that damn leg. Shit, they could have blown his arm off too and I would still be right there," Lay-Lay patted Tre's back as he squirmed in his stroller. "If that nigga would just let me show him the same kind of love he's shown me, then we would be all right. Last night I just got in my feelings too fast. Y'all think I wanna be sitting here with y'all ugly asses when I could be looking at Kyle? Hell nah! I should have stayed my behind right in Columbia last night."

Laughter serenaded their little corner as Lay-Lay spoke.

"Well take your butt back home. We ain't ask you to come in the first place," Morgan said

"Okay," Jade high-fived Morgan. "We just thought we'd take you out to eat so we could talk some sense into your dumb ass."

Lay-Lay looked at her girls and smiled. They were truly some characters. She was so glad to have them in her life. Their waiter had just brought out their burgers when a couple being seated in the corner across from them caught her eye.

"Well ain't this some shit? It must be blast from the past day or something." Lay-Lay pointed so Jade and Morgan could see what she was talking about.

"This nigga. Ain't you glad you left his ass?" Morgan asked, with her nose turned up.

Smoke was sitting down with some girl that wasn't Kristen. Not that they expected anything more from him, but it was still shocking. Now that they were no longer together, Lay-Lay could see just how stupid she used to look while she was with him. Kristen was at home knocked up with this nigga's second baby, and his ass had the nerve to be out to eat with the next bitch. The more Lay-Lay thought about it, the angrier she got. Before she knew it, she was out of her seat and headed for their table. When she got to it, Smoke looked shocked for a minute before smiling.

"What's up girl? When you got back in town?"

"Jaylen, who the hell is this?" The girl and Smoke both wore confused expressions. The girl spoke first.

"I'm Emoni. Who are you?"

"This nigga you out eating with has a family at home, shawty. You need to fall back."

The girl scrunched her face up before looking at Smoke. "A family? I thought you just got out of a bad relationship?" *Lawd, this dumb broad.* Lay-Lay shook her head.

"He did girl, with me. Now, he's with his kid's mother. They have a son and a baby girl on the way. He cheated on me the whole time we were together with her, so just letting you know; even if you continue seeing this little liar, he's going to fuck his baby mama whenever he gets ready to."

Smoke sat at the table with a smirk on his face, which only angered the girl. She slapped him upside his head before excusing herself from the table. When she walked away, Lay-Lay turned to do the same, only for Smoke to follow her back to their table.

"Lay-Lay, what did you take your ass over there and do?" Jade asked as Lay-Lay sat back down.

"Interrupted my damn lunch," Smoke sat in the empty chair next to Morgan.

"I just told his little date that he wasn't shit basically," Lay-Lay rolled her eyes and took a bite out of her burger.

"Lay-Lay, I swear you ain't got no sense at all," Morgan said.

Smoke leaned over the table and grabbed a fry out of her basket. "It's cool. She's the one I love anyway. Shit, maybe we can get back together now that I'm single again." He stroked her hand across the table.

Lay-Lay snatched it away like he'd just sat it on fire. "Nigga you must be crazy. That's something that a fool would do. I wish I would give your ass another chance. You'd be dead Jaylen, and you know it."

"Life ain't the same without you in it, Lay. I miss your ass. I ain't know I needed you this much." Smoke's mood was so somber that they almost felt sorry for him. Well, maybe Jade and Morgan did. Lay-Lay kept eating like she hadn't heard a word he said. "You hear me Lay-Lay?"

"You know I heard you, boy. We're at this little ass table. I just ain't stun you. You full of shit and I ain't got time for it. You should have thought about all of this before I got over you. The only thing you can get from me now is friendship, and as a friend I'm telling you, you better get Kristen. She's dumb as hell to keep putting up with your shit, but she loves your dog ass to death," Lay-Lay looked at him to make sure he was listening. "These days, unconditional love is hard to come by, so when you find it you better keep it."

"But I got unconditional love from you, too."

"Yeah you did. I just never got it from you, so I finally got some sense for myself and found me a man that was willing to give me back what I was giving him. I advise you to do the same."

Jade, Morgan, and Smoke looked at Lay-Lay as she shut whatever dreams Smoke had of them getting back together down, all the while eating her cheeseburger. She didn't look angry, hurt, amused or anything. She looked peaceful, something she hadn't been in years due to Smoke's crazy ass. Smoke wanted to object to what she was saying, but he couldn't. She was right. After they finished convincing him that he and Lay-Lay were never getting back together, they were able to enjoy the rest of their lunch. Smoke picked up the bill, and completed their good day. Lay-Lay had them drop her back off at the house so she could get back on the road. She didn't want to waste any time getting back to her man.

*****

Kyle's eyes flew to the door when he heard the locks turning. He was on the floor doing pushups when Lay-Lay walked in. She looked at him quickly before turning back around to lock the door. Although he knew they needed to talk, sex was on his mind. The way the light gray leggings she wore hugged her body, he could hardly push himself up from the floor again. Neither of them said anything; they just watched each other. Instead of going upstairs or sitting on the couch, Lay-Lay sat down Indian style in front of him on the floor. She held her hands in her lap as she watched him exercise.

Every time he pushed up, he would make eye contact with her, but every time he went down he was eyelevel with her thick thighs, and the soft, warm, love between them. Kyle tried to keep his mind off her wrapping her legs around him and moaning in his ear. She was going to want to talk about their problems first. Women always did.

Down...up...down...up...shit! This was hard to do. He needed to hurry up and talk so they could get to the making up.

"I woke up this morning with you on my mind, and you've been there ever since," Kyle said breathlessly.

"I don't want a divorce." Lay-Lay said it as if she was rushing to get it out.

"Neither do I, love. Having one leg is just really fucking with me right now."

"You do know I don't care about that, right?"

Kyle stopped doing pushups and sat back against the couch. He nodded his head and held his hand out to her. He pulled her onto his lap after she took it. He was wet from sweat, but it didn't look to be bothering her. He let his hands roam over her body a few times before bringing them up to her face. He pulled her head down and kissed her mouth. Her body relaxed in his arms as they conveyed intense passion through their lips. Lay-Lay started to grind her hips in a circle on his lap.

"Kyle pulled out of their kiss. "Hold up love, I'm dripping in sweat. Let me take a shower."

"No, I like you like this." Lay-Lay pulled her shirt over her head and attacked his mouth.

Kyle was in heaven as he reveled in the fact that his wife was back in his arms. After their little fight last night, he wasn't sure she would be coming back. He was glad she had.   The next morning, Kyle woke up to Lay-Lay's bright red hair in his face. Her entire body was sprawled across him, with her head on his chest. Her curls were directly in his eyes, some probably going up his nose. He inhaled her scent before kissing the top of her head. She stirred lightly as he caressed her back. When her head popped up, she was smiling at him. He smiled back as she leaned up so he could kiss her nose.

"Good morning my beautiful love."

"Morning baby."

"I'm sorry about our fight."

"I told you last night that we're good, babe." Lay-Lay got up from the bed and went into the bathroom. Kyle's eyes followed her. Along the way, she stopped and bent over. When she stood back up, she was holding the knob to their bathroom door. Her smiling face turned towards him.

"You probably should fix this," she snickered before continuing in the bathroom.

Kyle could hear the water from the sink running. He figured she was probably brushing her teeth, so he got up to join her. Lay-Lay was standing in the mirror looking at her body. She wore panties and nothing else. Kyle stood behind her and wrapped his arms around her waist.

"What you doing?"

"I'm fat."

Kyle shook his head and kissed her shoulder before walking over to turn the shower on. Lay-Lay watched him in the mirror.

"Why you shake your head?"

"Because I told you, you're not fat."

"Yes I am."

"Well, go to the gym with me today. We'll work out together."

Lay-Lay turned around and looked at him. "You'll help me work out?"

Kyle's face displayed that he couldn't believe she'd asked him something that dumb. "Of course."

"Well let's go now."

"Cool." Kyle flipped the shower off and went back into their room.

It took them a little over thirty minutes to get dressed and leave the house. Kyle stopped by the gas station to get Lay-Lay a Gatorade before going to the gym. When they walked in, Lay-Lay ended up grabbing more than just a Gatorade, but Kyle didn't mind. They were standing in line when Lay-Lay noticed the two girls behind them looking at Kyle whispering. It normally wouldn't have bothered her, because Kyle was fine as fuck–any woman that wasn't blind could see that–but these two bitches were different. They were looking at his leg. The thing that got her was that they were soldiers. If anybody understood his problems, it should have been them.

Kyle had on gym shorts, so you could see it with no problem. It had taken her nearly ten minutes to convince him to wear shorts, and now she could see why he hadn't wanted to. It was a good thing he wasn't paying the girls any mind. Knowing him, he probably would have played it off like it didn't bother him even if he had seen them. Lay-Lay, on the other hand, was pissed. She turned all the way around so that she was facing them, and crossed her arms over her chest.

"The fuck is y'all two bitches looking at?" Lay-Lay's voice was filled with malice. Kyle turned around as soon as he heard her talking.

"Excuse me?" the shortest one said.

"Bitch, you heard me. Y'all can't want y'all eyes anymore because if you did, you'd keep them to yourself."

Kyle turned all the way around and pulled Lay-Lay towards him. "It's all right mama, I'm good."

"I know you are. It's these two hoes that want their asses beat."

"We really don't know what you're talking about."

"Lie again so I can slap you. Y'all too old to be peeking and acting immature. Staring is for kids, scary ass bitches." Lay- Lay rolled her eyes before allowing Kyle to pull her from the store.

Kyle could tell she was fire hot. Her bright skin was turning red, and her eyebrows were damn near touching she had them frowned so hard. Although she didn't say it, he knew she had checked the girls about his leg. He expected people to look, but clearly Shalaya didn't. He was going to have to school his baby. She was on go at all times and although he appreciated it, she couldn't cuss out everybody that she caught looking at him. Once they were settled in the car, he looked over at her and placed his hand on her thigh. She was still breathing hard as she looked out of the window.

"Shalaya, look at me love." She shook her head no.

"Please." Her eyes were watering when she looked at him. "Why you crying, bae?"

He didn't know what it was, but as soon as he asked what was wrong, the flood broke and she started full out crying. She cried for a few minutes as he tried to get her to tell him what was wrong. When she was finally calm enough to tell him, he was a little taken aback at what she said.

"I don't want people looking at you, or whispering about you like something is wrong with you, because it's not. You're perfect and brave, and you don't deserve to be made fun of. I'm not going to have that. I promise you, I will put any and everybody I catch looking at you in their place." She was now crying again.

Kyle pulled into the parking space at the gym and parked before he leaned over and kissed her wet eyelids. "Listen love, I don't mind people looking. It's a part of our lives now. Let's just embrace it because contrary to what you may believe, I'm not perfect, and people are going to stare sometimes. It doesn't bother me, baby."

"Yes it does, Kyle. I know it does. So as long as I'm around, just know I'm checking everybody with wandering eyes that pause too long." Kyle laughed as he watched her wipe her eyes with the back of her hand.

"You talk all that shit, and you ain't nothing but a big crybaby."

"Shut up. No I'm not. I'm just not gon' play about you, and I have no problem letting them know it."

"Come on crybaby." Kyle kissed her lips before exiting the truck.

They walked into the gym, hand and hand. Lay-Lay was unsure of what to do first, so he helped her get onto the elliptical to do thirty minutes of cardio, while he got on the treadmill behind her. He left the pace low so he could get used to it with his leg. He made sure to stay where she could see him so she wouldn't get discouraged. They were both about fifteen minutes into their workout when another man working out got on the treadmill next to Kyle.

"Damn man, you got the best view in the house." The man's eyes lit up as he watched Lay-Lay's butt move around while she was on the machine. "She thick as grits, got damn!" The man's voice was filled with lust as he talked about Lay-Lay, unaware that she and Kyle were together.

"Bruh chill with all the disrespectful shit, that's my wife."

The guy's face changed from lust to uncertainty in an instant. He held his hands up in mock surrender. "Yo my fault man, I didn't know." Kyle didn't say anything he just nodded.

"She's a bad one though, bruh," the man said before walking away.

Kyle guessed he didn't want to work out right there anymore, being that he couldn't openly eye molest Lay-Lay. They stayed in their same place for another few minutes before Lay-Lay got off her machine and turned around to face him.

"You ready baby?"

"Yeah, you want to lift some weights?"

"Yeah, just make sure they ain't too heavy."

Kyle led Lay-Lay to the bottom floor, where the weights were. There was nothing but men down there, so he already knew they weren't staying long. Lay-Lay was already drawing attention, and all they were doing was walking.

"I ain't bringing your ass with me no more."

Lay-Lay looked up at him confused. "Why? What I do?"

"These niggas staring at your lil thick ass so damn hard they can hardly workout."

Lay-Lay scrunched her face up and looked around. Clearly, she hadn't been paying them any mind.

"I'll just get different workout clothes, maybe a bigger shirt or something."

Kyle shook his head. "Nah baby, you good. Niggas gon' be niggas no matter what you have on. It ain't like you could hide all that ass anyway."

Lay-Lay popped Kyle on the shoulder as he pulled her to the weight machine. He instructed her to duck so that the bar was on was on her shoulders. He removed some of the weights so that it wasn't too heavy for her before going back to stand behind her. He was so close on her that her butt was pressed against his growing manhood.

"What, you call yourself marking your territory right now or something?" Lay-Lay asked him as she looked at him through the mirror in front of them.

Kyle scrunched his face up as he looked at her. "What you talking 'bout?"

"You got your dick all on my butt. You must want these niggas to know all this ass belongs to you?" Lay-Lay wiggled a little bit so she was moving her butt on the slight erection he had.

"Stop playing girl." He slapped her butt hard before stepping back a little so she could do some squats.

Kyle instructed her on how to use the machine properly before leaving her to go lift some weights on his own. From where he was standing, he could still see her. He'd just sat up from doing some bench presses when he saw her speed walking towards him smiling. She was smiling so hard it practically touched her eyes. When she got closer to him, she started doing a cute little dance while she sang to him.

"You can tell everybody, yeah go ahead and tell everybody. You the man, you the man, you the man, yes you are, yes you are, yes you are."

Kyle didn't know he could smile so hard. The song was playing in the gym, and she was loving it. Lay-Lay had people looking at them as she stood there singing and dancing. She didn't care that she was drawing a crowd; all she was focused on was him. Her arms moved in sync with her body as she sang the lyrics to the music she'd deemed as his theme song. Her face was bright as her long, red hair hung down around her shoulders. The whole scene was cute as hell. When she was done, she ran up and jumped on him, wrapped her arms around his neck, and kissed his face. He had to grab the weight bar to keep them from falling.

"This is your song, baby! You're the man, baby. You're the man. I'm so proud of you." Lay-Lay was on her tiptoes trying to kiss him. Her arms had moved down to his waist and circled it as she held onto him.

Kyle marveled at her beautiful face. "I love you baby."

"I love you too babe, but let me get back to my workout. When I heard your song, I had to come sing it to you."

He watched her walk away with stars in his eyes. She was everything. She even turned back around as she was walking away and mouthed.

"You're the fucking man baby."

Kyle blew her a kiss and went back to his workout. He was talking about everybody else, but he didn't know if he could concentrate on working out as long as she was there either. They stayed for another hour before leaving. The married life was proving to be one worth living.

Chapter 10

Smoke looked down as the contact of another small person bumping into his leg jerked his body. Caleb looked up at him smiling. After scooping Caleb up into his arms, Smoke looked towards the front door of his barbershop. Kristen was walking in holding her belly. She was dressed in a teal-colored sundress with a trail of brown flowers around her waist. On her head was a flower crown headband that matched the belt. If he could, he'd keep her pregnant. It looked good on her. She had this natural glow that commanded attention from anybody close to her. She gave a weak smile when their eyes met.

"Hey daddy man. What you doing up here?" Smoke tickled Caleb's stomach.

"Care cut Daddyyyy," Caleb squealed, trying to say haircut.

Kristen stopped in front of Smoke's chair and sat down. She held her stomach while reaching to grab his Hydro flask off of his cutting station. She wasted no time untwisting the cap and drinking from it. Smoke just looked on in amusement.

"Damn girl, get your mouth off my shit. I ain't tell you to drink up my water." Smoke playfully grabbed at the cup. When she leaned back so he couldn't grab it, water spilled all over the front of her dress.

"Look what you made me do, Jaylen," Kristen grabbed the towel hanging from the arm of his chair and dabbed at her dress.

In all of the years he'd been with Kristen, he'd never liked for her to call him Jaylen, because that was reserved for Lay-Lay only. She was his main, and the only one with that privilege. He was Smoke to his side hoes and nothing more, but hearing Kristen call him Jaylen just then felt right. Maybe it was because he knew for a fact it was over with Lay-Lay, or maybe because she was no longer acting like a sidepiece. She made it clear he was to act accordingly, and until then there would be no "family time" for them. Smoke took the towel from her and tried to dry her himself.

"I'm sorry ma, let me help you."

"We're just making it worse. Just leave it alone," Kristen waved him off with her hand. "Caleb needs a haircut. I'm about to walk to the food court."

Smoke smiled as she rubbed her stomach. "Your fat ass. Stop feeding my baby all that unhealthy shit," Smoke checked the time on his watch. "How about I take you out to get some food. My next appointment isn't for another two hours."

Kristen started shaking her head no before he could even finish. "Nope, I think I'll pass."

"What? Why?"

"I'm not doing anything that might deepen my feelings for you; that includes going out to eat like we're a happy family."

"We are a happy family, Kris. You just don't know it yet."

"Nah nigga, I already believed that before and you played me. Not happening again." Kristen got up from his chair and leaned over to kiss Caleb. Before she could pull away, Smoke grabbed her arm and pulled her to him. He kissed her long and hard. He was happy when she didn't pull back. This showed him that he still had a chance. When he finally released her lips, she turned her head and grabbed her chest as if she needed to catch her breath. "I'ma give your ass one more chance, but this is it."

Smoke smiled and grabbed her hand.

"Now take me to feed my baby, please." Kristen winked at him as she waited for him to grab his phone and wallet from his drawer.

Once he stuck it in his pocket, he grabbed her hand and kissed it.

"Lord, you in your feelings hard today, huh? Kissing my hand and stuff."

"See, why I can't be nice? Let me let your lil hand go before you have something else smart to say," Smoke threw her hand down, only for her to grab his right back.

"Nooooo, I'm just playing, baby daddy. Hold it again." Kristen's smile was infectious.

Smoke held her hand with one hand and Caleb in the other as they exited the mall. Kristen was craving fried rice, so they chose to go to Benihana for lunch. The entire ride was fun and relaxing. They talked about a little bit of everything, including the women that he'd cheated on her with. Surprisingly, she didn't even get mad. She only listened and asked questions when she wanted to. Her nonchalant demeanor made it easier for him to tell her everything.

She stressed to him that this would be the only way that they could have a fresh start. Smoke understood, so he told as much as he could without hurting her feelings. Being truthful was cool, but some stuff was better left unsaid. Although she was acting like she could handle everything, he was smart enough to know that anything he said today would most likely be used in an argument later on down the road. By the time they pulled into the restaurant, Caleb had fallen asleep. Smoke scooped him up in one arm before grabbing Kristen in the other. Doing the family thing actually felt kind of nice. Once they were seated, they ordered their food and continued their conversation from the car.

"So, me and Lay-Lay were the only two you ever loved?" Kristen didn't look like she believed him.

"Yeah. I don't know why that's so hard for you to believe."

"It's hard to believe because it seems like we're the two you did the worst."

Smoke thought about what she said, and a smile spread across his face. "That is kind of fucked up, ain't it?"

"Uh yeah." Kristen looked at him like he should have already known the answer to that.

"Y'all two don't let a nigga breathe, that's why. Y'all two have gots to have the worst mouths in the history of nagging females."

"You still love her, don't you?"

Smoke sat quietly and nodded his head as he took a sip of his water.

"You in love with her?"

Again, he nodded.

"Well, that's good for your ass. It don't feel good to be in love with somebody and have to watch them be with somebody else, does it?"

"Nah,"

"I know it don't. Maybe now you'll learn how to treat people. Hell, I'm happy for the girl. After seeing the condition you had her in, she deserves something good. Your ass wasn't good for her. I hope they stay married forever."

"You must be trying to piss me off or something?"

Kristen shook her head and scooted back so the server could place their food on the table.

"I really feel like you are."

"Listen Jaylen, I'm not trying to piss you off, I'm simply stating how I feel. I just sat here and listened to you tell me about all the women you've fucked and didn't say a word, so don't get in your feelings now because I'm talking about Lay-Lay. I can be happy for her if I want to. I know how it feels to be dirted by your ass." Kristen stuck a fork full of rice and chicken into her mouth. "All I'm saying baby daddy, is it's time to move on. Everything isn't always about you. Instead of thinking about Smoke all the time, think about Jaylen for a change. Think about Caleb and Cailyn; you're getting too old for all these games you play."

Smoke hadn't thought about none of the stuff Kristen was saying until she said it. He honestly didn't think she had enough sense to think like an adult. He'd been underestimating her all these years, or maybe he hadn't paid her enough attention to see that she really was a good woman. He watched her stick a spoon of rice into Caleb's mouth, and his heart warmed. Maybe she could be the woman to make him change. She'd been patiently waiting for years to be his only. He owed her and his kids a chance to completely have him.

"What about you Kris, can I think about you too?" He noticed she hadn't said her name earlier when listing the people he should think about.

"If you want to."

"Well I want to."

"We'll see. Right now I have to pee." Kristen slid out of her chair and went to the restroom.

She knew it was time for her to have Cailyn because she was weighing on her bladder a little too much these days. It seemed like every time she got comfortable, she had to get right back up and pee. She stood in the mirror, fingering her hair to make sure it was still intact. If it was one thing she hated, it was an ugly pregnant woman. She couldn't stand to see pregnant women that let themselves go. Once she was satisfied with herself, she washed her hands. She looked in the mirror at the woman that had just come into the bathroom. She smiled at her and continued washing her hands.

"You're here with Smoke?" the girl stood next to her and asked.

Kristen was sure the look on her face displayed how uninterested she was in the conversation the girl was trying to have.

"Yes I am."

"Is he the father of your baby?"

"Yes bitch damn, why?" Kristen was not in the mood for any foolishness, pregnant or not.

"I just thought you should know he and I are together."

Kristen laughed at her and shook her head. This hoe was crazy. If her and Smoke were together, then why in the hell was she talking to her instead of her so-called man?

"Okay, good for y'all. Now excuse me I have to go." Kristen tried to walk past her, but she stepped in front of her.

"Girl, if you don't get your ass out my way."

"What you gon' do? Tell Smoke?"

"Nope, I'ma beat your ass all around this fucking bathroom."

That statement must have pissed her off something terrible, because she rushed Kristen and slammed her into the wall behind them. Kristen cocked back and punched her in the face repeatedly as she tried to pin her to the wall. She stayed low, almost like she was hiding from Kristen's blows. It was like she wasn't even focused on the fight anymore. It didn't dawn on Kristen was she was doing until she felt a hard blow to her stomach. Kristen grew strength out of nowhere and pushed her so hard she flew across the bathroom. This didn't deter her, because she right back on her.

Kristen leaned over, trying to protect her baby from this lunatic. She balled up as tight as she could and screamed to the top of her lungs. Maybe somebody would hear her. As bad as she wanted to fight this girl back, she needed to protect her daughter more, because that's who she was aiming for.

"I will have him to myself. I'm tired of sharing him with all of you side bitches and y'all bastard ass babies." The unknown girl drew back and kicked Kristen as hard as she could in the side of her head.

That kick hurt like hell, but she wasn't about to cave that easy. Cailyn needed her. The girl continued to kick and punch her. Kristen felt herself getting weaker, so she had to think fast. The next time the girl's foot came up, she grabbed it and pushed her backwards. As soon as she lost her footing, Kristen pushed her with all of her might into the sink and punched her again. While she fought to get to her, Kristen made a run for the door. She managed to get out of it, but the girl was still on her. She had a handful of Kristen's hair, trying to drag her back in the bathroom.

"JAYLEN!" Kristen yelled across the restaurant.

Her scream caught the attention of patrons that were sitting close to them. A few people jumped up to help her, but none of them were moving faster than Smoke. She could see him running towards her with Caleb in his arms. She could still feel the vicious blows the girl was landing to the back of her head, but it didn't matter because Smoke was about to save her. He was starting to become blurry as her vision clouded. Her body got weaker and weaker before collapsing to the floor.

*****

The loud ringing of King's phone startled Jade as she sat in the corner trying to read. King and baby King were asleep on the bed, so she hopped up to grab the phone before it could wake either of them up. It was Smoke.

"Hey Smoke, what's going on?"

"Aye, where King at?" His voice sounded frantic.

"He right here. What's going on? You okay?"

"Yeah ma I'm good, but shit is all bad right now. Lana's dumb ass attacked Kristen at Benihana's today while we was out eating. They're about to do an emergency C-section on Kris to get the baby, because her heart rate was dropping too fast after Kristen's water broke," Smoke paused for a moment before continuing. "Aye, I need y'all to come to the hospital with me man. I can't handle this shit. They got Kristen hooked up to different shit, she's pretty fucked up too." Smoke sounded defeated.

"Just calm down Smoke, we'll be there in a minute. Where's Caleb?"

"Her sister has him. We're at Grady."

"Okay, try to stay positive, we'll be there in a minute." Jade hung up the phone and went to wake King up. As soon as she told him what was going on, he jumped up. She dressed baby King while King got himself together. Once they were in the car, she called Morgan and Lay-Lay on three way. She went in as soon as they were all connected.

"Y'all, why this crazy bitch Lana dun took her coo-coo ass to Benihana while Smoke and Kristen was eating and attacked the damn girl in the bathroom?"

"Shut up Jade! Are you serious?" Morgan was too outdone.

"Oh my God, is she okay?" Lay-Lay's voice was filled with concern.

"They had to rush her to the hospital because her water broke during the fight. Lil mama's heartbeat started dropping, so they're doing a C-section. We're headed up there now."

Morgan sighed. "Well me and Dallas will meet y'all up there."

"Y'all keep me updated. I hope they be all right. Tell Smoke I said I'm praying for them and to call me if he needs anything." Lay-Lay was just as worried as her friends.

Jade told them she would talk to them later, because they had just pulled into the hospital's parking lot. King grabbed baby King's carrier from the backseat and they rushed towards the entrance. When they got to the labor and delivery floor, they saw Kristen's sister sitting next to the window with Caleb in her lap. When he saw her, he jumped from her lap and ran straight to Jade.

"Tee-Tee!" He smiled with his arms stretched up towards her.

When Jade picked him up, she didn't miss the dirty look Kristen's sister gave her. It was no secret that she didn't like Jade, which was cool because Jade didn't like her ass either. She rolled her eyes at King when he pulled Jade's arm towards the chairs so they could sit down. As bad as Jade wanted to say something, she chose not to because now wasn't the time.

King turned towards Kristen's sister. "Aye, have they told y'all anything else?"

"Nah, the baby should be here soon though. They've been back there for a while."

"How's Kristen?" Jade asked, trying to be cordial.

"She straight."

Attitude dripped from every word that she spoke. Jade just laughed and turned back around. When King had been talking to her, she talked like she had some sense. Another thirty minutes passed before Smoke came walking from the back in a scrub gown and hat. Dallas, Morgan, and the twins had gotten there about ten minutes after Jade and King, and they were all waiting to check on Kristen and baby Cailyn. When they saw Smoke, Jade and Morgan rushed to him trying to see was everything okay.

"How's Kristen and the baby?" Morgan asked.

"They're good. Cailyn is going to have to stay in the NICU for a little while because she's not breathing on her own yet, and she needs to gain more weight, but everything else is fine. Kris is a little bruised up, but she straight too," Smoke said before hugging both of the women.

Kristen's sister walked up with Caleb on her hip. "Can we see her or the baby?"

"Not yet, she's still in surgery. We can go see Cailyn in minute once they get her settled."

It was a weight lifted from them all as they heard the good news. Cailyn was two months early, so she was only two pounds. Other than that, everything was good. Jade was too happy. She called Lay-Lay to let her know what was going on while they waited to see Kristen and the baby. It was funny to Jade how just a few months ago they all hated Kristen, and now they were all worried about her. It's funny how things change the more you mature.

Jade handed baby King to King when it was time to go see the baby. He whined a little as King placed him against his chest and patted his back. He turned his little head from side to side, trying to get comfortable on his daddy's chest. King hummed softly and he settled down almost immediately, like he always did. King hummed to him all day every day. It was the cutest thing. Whenever baby King heard his father's voice, he would squirm and fidget until he picked him up. King walked next to Dallas, where he was standing with the twins in their double stroller. Tre was knocked out while little Miss. nosey Daylen was wide-awake.

"We'll go see Cailyn first. Kristen is still a little high on her meds." Smoke led them down the hallway to the NICU. "We're going to have to take turns. Two at a time. I've already seen her, so y'all go ahead."

"King and I will go first," Jade volunteered. She heard Kristen's sister suck her teeth in the background. "Here Smoke, get my baby." Jade took baby King from King and passed him to Smoke.

They washed their hands, and Jade removed her jewelry before they were allowed access. The room that Cailyn was in was filled with babies. It was dark and very quiet, minus some talking from the nurses. Her little incubator was in the far corner with a pink blanket thrown over the top of it. She had a small tube up her nose with a little yellow knitted hat on her head. Another yellow blanket was thrown loosely across her. She was lying on her back with both of her arms above her head.

"She's so precious babe, look at her." Jade stuck her hands in the two little arm holes on her crib and rubbed her legs. Cailyn jumped from the contact and began to stir around. Jade tried to calm her down by rubbing her, but she wasn't having it.

"Watch out bae, let me touch her." King walked over and replaced Jade's hands with his. He stroked Cailyn's feet, then her stomach. She kept moving and making little noises.

"You guys can hold her if you would like." The nurse came over and began taking Cailyn out of her little crib. She placed a gown over King's chest since he wanted to hold her first, and handed Cailyn to him. She offered him the rocking chair, but he declined and chose to stand. Cailyn's little body looked even smaller as she lay on King's chest. Jade watched how gentle he was being with her and fell in love all over again. He rubbed her back slowly before singing Usher's verse from him and Wale's song "Matrimony."

"You singing that to the baby?" Jade smiled.

"I don't know any baby songs."

King went back to singing as Jade stood by and watched. Cailyn responded the same way baby King did. She laid her head down and fell off to sleep. They stayed for a few more minutes before leaving so the others could come in. When they got outside, Dallas was holding Daylen while Morgan had baby King. Jade grabbed him and kissed his head full of curls.

"Smoke, King in there trying to take your baby. He started singing and her lil butt had the nerve to stop crying."

"No she didn't," Morgan laughed.

"Yeah, that lil heffa cried when I touched her. Smoke better get ready, because she already fast. As soon as that man touched her, she shut her lil mouth and went to sleep."

Smoke slapped King's back. "Jade, my boy needs a daughter."

"I keep trying to tell her," King cosigned.

"Um, y'all can shut up. Our baby ain't event that old yet. I need a minute."

They all stood around talking for a little while longer, until it was time to see Kristen. They were happy to see she was doing better, minus a few bruises from the fight. She even seemed happy to see all of them there checking on her. It was almost seven that night by the time Jade, King, and the baby left the hospital. Jade was so tired; all she wanted to do was crawl in her bed, and that's exactly what she did the moment they got home.

Chapter 11

Lay-Lay was lying across the bed watching TV when Kyle walked in the room on the phone. He looked like the conversation he was having was a disturbing one. His face was frowned as he sat on the edge of the bed. Lay-Lay watched him, waiting for him to get off the phone. When he finally got off, he turned around to face her.

"You'll never guess who that was."

"Who?"

"Jones. His wife is in jail for aggravated assault and some other stuff for jumping on a pregnant girl."

Lay-Lay sat up and slapped Kyle's arm. "You are so slow sometimes, Kyle. I just told you last night that she had jumped on Smoke's babymama."

Kyle's eyes got big as he snapped his fingers. "You sure did. Damn, I ain't even put that shit together. That's fucked up."

"So what is he going to do?"

"He said he's leaving her ass down there. She was fighting over another nigga; that's all he needed to hear and he's ready to divorce her ass now."

"It's about time. It took his ass long enough."

Lay-Lay shook her head and laid back down on the bed. Kyle stretched out beside her and ended up falling asleep snuggled up against her. Lay-Lay watched him sleep and reveled in happiness. This was what life was supposed to be like. Happiness every day. Tired herself, Lay-Lay slid down until she was lying on his chest, and she too fell asleep.

It was dark outside by the time they woke up. Kyle woke up first, because his phone was ringing. It was his company commander letting him know that he was being awarded the Purple Heart, and would have to attend a ceremony for it. He was elated to be receiving an honor of that caliber. He risked his life every day while on deployment; it felt good to have his efforts acknowledged. He was so excited he had to wake Lay-Lay up and share the good news.

He shook her lightly. "Shalaya, wake up." She swatted at his hand with her face frowned up.

"Bae, get up. I got some good news."

"What is it?" Lay-Lay asked with her eyes still closed.

"I'm getting the Purple Heart award."

Lay-Lay's eyes shot open as she dove on top of him. She smothered his face with kisses as he laughed.

"You deserve it baby. You really do."

Kyle hugged her tighter and fell back onto the bed, bringing her with him. She squealed and laughed until he began kissing her neck. Nothing would top off his good news like being wrapped in his wife's love.

*****

Three weeks later...

It was the day of Kyle's award ceremony, and their house was in all kinds of disarray. All of their friends and family was there, and had been for the entire weekend. They'd all wanted to get hotel rooms, but Kyle's extra family-oriented ass wanted everybody to stay at the house. Initially Lay-Lay had been against it, because everybody had kids and needed space, but he insisted. His parents, King and Jade, Dallas and Morgan, Zion and TaSheena, even Smoke and Kristen had come– not to mention all five of the babies were there. Their house was packed to the max, but she had to admit it had been fun. When Kyle told her to invite Smoke and Kristen, she thought he had lost his mind, but it turned out to be one of the best ideas he'd ever had. It gave Lay-Lay and Kristen time to clear the air, and get acquainted with each other the right way. She repeatedly told him no when he told her to invite them, until Morgan and Jade agreed it might be a good idea, being that Smoke was a part of their circle. Hannah and Arlington were in hog heaven with all the babies in the house. They smothered all of the babies with love; you would have thought all of them were their grandkids. Overall, having everyone there to help Kyle celebrate was enjoyable.

"Bae, where my beret?" Kyle asked, referring to the hat that he wore with his uniform.

Lay-Lay, Hannah, Morgan, Jade, Kristen, and Tasheena were all in the kitchen feeding the babies when he walked in. He was already dressed in his uniform and looking sexier than ever.

"Oh Lord, somebody come pick me up off the floor. My baby looking so good I'm getting weak in the knees," Lay-Lay fanned herself as she eyed Kyle up and down. He was in his dress Blues, which was the formal Army uniform. Various colors of ranks and awards were pinned to it, making the dark blue jacket stand out even more.

Kyle blushed from her comment. "Thanks beautiful." Kyle held his head down, trying to suppress his smile as Lay-Lay drooled over him.

"Y'all are so cute!" Tasheena said, looking between the two of them.

"Ain't they though?" Kristen said.

Lay-Lay smiled at them as she walked over to Kyle and wrapped her arms around his waist. "You give me a kiss, and I'll tell you where your hat is"

Kyle leaned down and slid his tongue deep into her mouth. He rubbed his hands up and down her back as they kissed.

"Well I guess we ain't sitting here," Hannah said, making them break their lip lock.

They both laughed nervously as they pulled apart. He left, and she followed him from the kitchen and into the living room to grab his hat. The other men were sitting in there dressed and waiting on the women. When Lay-Lay saw them, she hurried up and ran back to the kitchen to tell the ladies they needed to get a move on. It took another thirty minutes for everyone to get completely ready to leave the house. They pulled up to the center where Kyle's ceremony was being held four cars deep.

They were ushered inside and showed to their assigned seats. Hannah had insisted everyone wear white, so they drew pretty much everyone's attention as they walked in. Caleb, baby King, and Tre were all dressed alike, while Daylen and Cailyn wore the same little dresses with flower crowns on their heads. People could hardly concentrate on anything once the children came in. They were all so cute you couldn't help but to stare at them. After everyone was seated, Lay-Lay and Kyle made their way to the stage.

Lay-Lay was dressed in a white bandage dress that hung loosely from one shoulder, with all of her hair pulled into a French braid going diagonal down the back of her head. Happiness radiated off her as she made her way through the room holding Kyle's hand. Kyle helped her onto the stage before following her. They took their seats in front of his company. There were all there dressed in their ACU's. Lay-Lay was still getting used to the Army life, but it was growing on her. Some things still caught her off guard, such as the way they all stood up and saluted him as he walked past. Kyle saluted them back and acted as if it was no big deal.

Thankfully, the ceremony started on time and everything was moving along. Lay-Lay's eyes wandered over to her family as she sat next to Kyle on the small stage. Morgan and Jade smiled and blew her kisses, while King and Dallas sat close by. Hannah was smiling with tears in her eyes as Arlington looked on in admiration. Smoke winked at her and gave a light head nod, while Kristen was busying feeding Cailyn. Tasheena and Zion were busy looking around the room in amazement. She couldn't describe the love she felt for all of them at the moment if she had to. It was too overwhelming.

Kyle squeezed her hand lightly, letting her know it was almost time for him to receive his honorary award. She smiled and nodded her head at Arlington. He was going to aid in the presentation of Kyle's Purple Heart. Being that Arlington was retired military himself, Kyle wouldn't have had it any other way. He walked to the stage just as Kyle and Lay-Lay were summoned to the center of the stage. Kyle stood first and turned to help her from her seat. Before he even moved to walk, he leaned down to kiss her. The crowd swooned at his act of affection.

Lay-Lay's heart was beating out of her chest; she was so nervous. Her heart was beating so loud she couldn't hear anything that was being said. All she saw was the man hand Arlington the gold medal with the purple ribbon tied to it. Arlington and Kyle both stood at attention and saluted one another before Arlington pinned it to Kyle's jacket. Tears streamed down Lay-Lay's face as she watched the water gather in Arlington's eyes. Approbation and reverence was written all over his face as he leaned forward and embraced Kyle. When he pulled away, he kissed Lay-Lay's cheek and left the stage.

"Is there anything you would like to say, Major Taylor?" the man asked as he handed Kyle the mic.

Kyle grabbed it. "Thank you all. I am extremely humbled and grateful for this honor. Serving my country hasn't always been easy, but I can definitely say it has been worth it. Being able to save lives is a blessing, and one of my greatest gifts from God. I'll never take my job, nor will I take my ability to protect and serve, for granted." Kyle stretched his arm out in the direction of their family. "Secondly, I would like to thank my family for being here to support me on this day. You guys are amazing, and I love and appreciate you."

The crowd clapped for a minute before calming back down to allow him to finish talking. Once the room was quiet again, Kyle turned to Lay-Lay and smiled.

"I don't even know where to start when it comes to this woman. She has been everything I never knew I needed. Losing my leg has been one of the most difficult times in my life. I've had some days where I wished I would have died in the explosion, and I've had some days where I want to rip of this prosthesis and never look at it again, but through it all, she's been there. Every minute of every day, she's been my lover, my friend, my support system, my rock, and my world," Kyle paused for a minute when his voice cracked with tears. It took him a few seconds to gain his composure, but he eventually got it. "I don't know if I would have ever made it through any of this without you, Shalaya. You kept me sane and when I was ready to throw it all away, you wouldn't let me. You are the truly the best part of me. It's because of you that I'm standing here today." Kyle grabbed her face with both of his hands "You're my rib, Shalaya Taylor, and I promise to love you with everything I have. Thank you all once again." Kyle handed he microphone back to the man in charge as the building erupted in applause.

Lay-Lay looked around the room at all of the people there to support Kyle. Her face was already wet with tears from Kyle's speech, but it got even worse then. She didn't know how she'd lucked up and found a man that loved her the way Kyle did. This was a life she'd been dreaming and praying about since she could remember, and it was finally here. Everything she'd asked God for had finally come true. The rest of the program went by swiftly. Before she knew it, it was over and she and Kyle were about to walk off stage, but there was one last thing that needed to be done. She looked to the back of the room and nodded her head. Aloe Blacc's song "The Man" came through the speakers.

Kyle looked down at her and smiled. "You told them to play this?"

"Yep! You're the man baby," Lay-Lay smiled so hard her cheeks were hurting, but the smile that was on his face was definitely worth it. "One more thing, Major Taylor."

"What's that baby?"

"You're also the father." Kyle's face scrunched up in confusion before that big beautiful smile crept back on it.

"We're having a baby?"

"Yes sir we are, in about seven more months."

Kyle's arms went around her, squeezing her tightly into his chest. "Damn baby, I love you so much."

"I love you too baby."

Kyle and Lay-Lay walked off the stage and over to their loved ones to share the good news. They were all just as excited as they were. Everyone began to pour out of the building, with Lay-Lay falling behind a few steps. She looked at all of her friends and family. This was love. This was the life she never wanted to stop living.

The End

Join our mailing list to get a notification when Leo Sullivan Presents has another release!

Text LEOSULLIVAN to 22828

to join!

Last release:

<u>This Thug Put A Move On My Heart</u>

Check out our new and upcoming releases on the next page! Click the new releases image below to read for FREE with Kindle Unlimited

To submit a manuscript for our review, email us at leosullivanpresents@gmail.com

Join our mailing list to get a notification for these upcoming releases!

CPSIA information can be obtained
at www.ICGtesting.com
Printed in the USA
LVHW081829081219
639822LV00015B/817/P